Stone of Destiny

Mary L. Ball

Copyright © 2013 Mary L.Ball

ALL RIGHTS RESERVED

Cover Art by Joan Alley

This book is a work of fiction and any resemblance to persons, living or dead, or places, events or locales is purely coincidental. The characters are the product of the author's imagination and used fictitiously.

Warning: The unauthorized reproduction or distribution of this copyrighted work is illegal. No part of this book may be scanned, uploaded, or distributed via the Internet or any other means without the permission of Prism Book Group. Please purchase only authorized editions and do not participate in the electronic piracy of copyrighted material. Thank you for respecting the hard work of this author.

STONE OF DESTINY © 2013 Mary L. Ball
Published by Prism Book Group
ISBN 978-1-940099-15-6 First Edition, 2013
Published in the United States of America
Contact info: contact@prismbookgroup.com
http://www.prismbookgroup.com

"'Truly I tell you, if anyone says to this mountain, "Go, throw yourself into the sea," and does not doubt in their heart but believes that what they say will happen, it will be done for them.'" Mark 11:23 (NIV)

DEDICATION

To my Grandson Dalton—"D"— whose fascination with magic sparked my desire to write about a spiritual kind of magic that happens with faith and prayer.

PROLOGUE

AN UNEXPECTED SOUND woke Elizabeth. The faint click-clatter traveled up the steps toward the bedroom, where she cuddled beside her husband. Straining her senses, she tried to figure out what caused the noise. Elizabeth was about to close her eyes again when a second commotion jerked them open. As she turned over on her back, she remembered the yellow-striped tabby downstairs. Tiger had grown full of fun in the last few months, always finding something to frolic with or climb on.

When another fleeting rattle reached her ears, Elizabeth thought of the plastic cup she had drunk water from hours before, left out on the counter. The seven-month-old kitten was playfully batting the cup around. Letting out a sigh, she tossed back the covers, knowing if she didn't quiet the little fellow, she wouldn't get any sleep tonight.

Paul Harrison woke as she yawned and stretched. Reaching out, he took hold of her hand. "Stay put. I'll go downstairs and check on things. Baby animals can be ornery. I'll lock Tiger in the pantry."

He gave her a quick kiss, rolled sideways, and threw his legs over the bed as he sat. Slipping his feet into house slippers, he seemed to fight exhaustion with an arm stretch and walked toward the hallway. Another bang and clatter rent the air. Paul trotted into the dark passage.

Elizabeth adjusted her pillow and propped in a sitting position against the headboard. She reached over and pushed the switch to the lamp on the wooden side table. Their wedding photo alighted. Smiling to herself, she ran her hand across the quilt on her bed, admiring the blue and red ring pattern. Red was her favorite color, Paul's blue. Paul's younger sister Kay had spent months sewing the coverlet as a gift. The teenager had put in a lot hard work to make it perfect.

Smoothing down the bed linen, Elizabeth smiled at her wedding band and the heirloom ring she wore on her right hand. The sapphire shined a deep, dark blue and sparkled, despite the intense color. The gem seemed to emanate a bright glow from within.

She moved her hand closer and dim light captured the pigment in the crystal. The stone twinkled like a hundred miniature stars. Elizabeth sighed, soaking in the beauty of the jewelry as she removed it from her finger.

What a happy life she'd married into.

Rubbing the smooth surface of the stone, she recalled her wedding day as well as the day she first met her husband.

Paul was so handsome…he'd been walking past her sister's street at the very same time she happened to be checking the mail. He tipped his hat toward her in greeting, and she nodded a hello.

They later laughed about the incident when Paul told her the only reason he'd been strolling through the neighborhood was because his car ran out of gas, leaving him stranded to find the nearest station.

On summer vacation, Elizabeth was planning to return home—two states away. Then Paul asked her to come to the church bazaar. Without hesitating, she delayed her trip to accompany him.

God truly works in mysterious ways.

Leaning against the headboard, Elizabeth once more eyed the ring her mother-in-law had given her. The two of them spent the afternoon shopping together while she listened to anecdotes of unique guidance. Elizabeth clutched the gold hoop, studying the stone. *My mother-in-law had visions that led her to find Paul when he was a little boy and lost in a hidden cave. She was wearing this ring. Never before had she experienced any premonitions.* Elizabeth continued to speculate about the women in past generations who had worn the charm. So many wonderful stories of prayers answered…

With her hand scrunched tight against her chest, she spent the next few seconds thanking the Lord for her blessings and her husband.

She had to be the luckiest woman alive.

Elizabeth's mind raced ahead as she envisioned the household she hoped to have one day. Love and happiness flowed from her heart and bubbled up like water boiling on a stove.

She meditated on God's words about faith. To her way of thinking, a lot of the good things that happened in life were because she believed in the Lord's promises. As she closed her eyes in prayer, adoration and gratitude seeped from a hopeful bride's heart. Saying "Amen," she then recited her favorite Bible verse in First Corinthians, which speaks of love, being patient and kind.

A thunderous crash boomed through her prayers. A shot rang out in the air.

A gun shot! She grabbed her throat as her eyes flashed open. Before she could dart from under the quilt, unsure where to flee, she heard the scuffle of footsteps outside the bedroom door. Elizabeth shrieked in horror as a man flung open the door and lunged toward the bed. A black mask covered his face and stone-cold eyes gleamed with hatred through the peepholes of the head covering.

Her body quaked with fear. The grip she had on the ring fell away, and the band slipped out of her hand, falling on the floor as Elizabeth screamed in terror.

A blast sounded. Blackness closed in around her, leaving only the stilled silence of death.

CHAPTER ONE

Fifty years later...

PARKED OFF THE side of the road, Taylor sunk into the soft leather seat of her red sports car, massaging a headache as she hissed out instructions to her assistant. *For goodness sake, I don't often ask Dave to stay late. Would the man die of starvation if he didn't make it home by six for supper with his family?* Taking a hard breath, she ended the conversation she'd pulled over to complete. Teeth clenched, she hit the steering wheel in frustration.

With a heavy sigh, Taylor turned and gazed out the side window. The vibrant sight of a purple wisteria in full bloom lifted her spirits. Across the road, pink and white azaleas were coming into bud. Spring was indeed once again poking out its head—her favorite time of the year. As she pulled into traffic, she tilted her head against the afternoon sun, letting the warmth bathe her face.

Taylor Harrison was the youngest-ever chief executive officer over operations at Mugful's Corporation. Four years ago, she'd started in the marketing department, promoting the assorted hot beverages. When old man Zimmerman, the owner of the company, retired, his nephew Jack took over the operations. Soon after, she was promoted to a supervisory position. Her career had accelerated from there. For the past year, her newest duties had her working long hours. To Taylor, the rewards were worth the sacrifices. Late nights paved her way. The North Carolina division within the hot drink company was now out of the red. Stores slated to close were revived. Taylor was proud. Her territory was on top.

If Dave aspired to ever be more than a coffee-fetcher, he'd do well to mimic her example. There was a price to pay for success.

Maneuvering through the city traffic in Raleigh, Taylor drove past a government complex. A quick right turn set her on a road toward a well-maintained residential section of town. The condominium she called home was only a few blocks from the corporate branch of Mugful's. One of the reasons she was attracted to the area.

Parking in the cobblestone drive, she checked her reflection in the rear-view mirror. Taylor ran her fingers through her upswept shoulder-length hair to smooth down the ringlets. Straightening her thick chestnut tresses was something she had given up on. The last thing Taylor had time for was being obsessed with well-behaved hair. Keeping a short style made getting ready for work an even harder chore, and she hated using gel. Thus, Taylor's morning routine mainly consisted of her piling her natural curls in a bun or using a hair barrette.

While she gathered her briefcase from the front seat, the sound of a beach tune blared from inside her handbag. Shutting her car door, she dug through her purse, feeling past her checkbook and lipstick for her cell phone. Taylor glanced at the front and smiled at the name lit up on the screen. "Hi, Granny Kay."

A gentle voice sounded from the other end and wrapped around Taylor like a blanket. Kay Harrison was the only person who could melt her heart in an instant. She had spent most of her younger years with her father's mother. Dad's job required him to travel a lot, and her mother chose to accompany him on most of his trips. Because her parents were away more often than not, she had built a close bond with her grandmother. The love she felt for the older woman was unconditional. She would do anything to please Granny Kay.

Taylor pictured her grandmother sitting in her chair, dressed in her usual attire of khakis and a button-up blouse. Endowed with the same kinky locks as Taylor, she wore her ringlets cut short.

After they exchanged pleasantries, there was an awkward pause. Taylor noted the silence, one of her grandmother's mannerisms. The hesitation signified she wanted to ask a favor. For as long as Taylor could remember, her grandmother wavered when she was going to request something from someone.

"Taylor, I'm going to sell my house," the older woman finally proclaimed in a no-nonsense tone.

"You are? Why?"

Granny Kay listed her reasons for shedding the extra burden the big house now caused.

"I see…uh-huh. True…" Listening attentively, Taylor juggled her briefcase and purse as she approached the front door of her condominium. "No, I can't argue with you there."

As her grandmother continued to speak, Taylor unlocked the big red door and walked inside. She tossed her black leather purse on the marble table and then laid the case holding her laptop on the granite bar separating her living room from the kitchen.

Strolling into the eating area, Taylor reached in the refrigerator for a bottle of water as she concentrated on the words flowing in the slow, southern draw her grandmother used.

Taylor sipped her water and then waited for her grandmother to exhaust her speech about the trials of the family house.

"But aren't you staying at your friend's only temporarily? What if you decide to move back home once the broken hip heals?"

"Hun, you know that since your grandpa died, it's just me in that big ole place. I'm not the woman I used to be. Age has begun to take its toll. My fall down those stairs proves I need a change. No, the place is much too big for me to live in by myself anymore. I had always planned for you to have it as your home one day. We could live there together. I know we wouldn't get in each other's way."

Taylor set her bottle on the counter and crossed her arm over her chest, rubbing her shoulder. She didn't want the conversation to veer in this direction. Residing in Raleigh was a decision she'd made long ago. She preferred to be in a modern city and close to work.

Though Taylor spent a lot of years growing up in the family house, it wasn't what she wanted. No, as much as she loved her grandmother, living with her in a big, creaky Victorian was not an option she cared to entertain.

"Granny Kay, you know I work long hours most of the time. It's dark before I get home. Liberty Cove is an hour's drive. I'm afraid I wouldn't be much help." Taylor pushed a strand of hair behind her ear, guilt threatening. "I know you always wanted me to have the family house one day. But it's not my style. The upkeep of a vintage home and the big yard would be too much. I enjoy simple condominium living."

"I know you do, dear."

In an attempt to lighten the mood, she changed her tone and added a slight chuckle, "Sometimes I think I use my apartment just to sleep in. With the hours I put in at the office, living here is more convenient."

There was a momentarily silence before her grandmother cleared her throat. "You work all the time, hun. I wish you would slow down, maybe give some thought to a family."

Taylor rubbed her mouth, her face twisted in discomfort. Biding time before she answered, she took a sip of water. "A husband isn't what I want. Not right now. I have my career to think about."

The clinking sound of ice came through the phone, causing Taylor to picture her grandmother holding a glass of sweetened tea. For as long as she could remember, the woman had been a true southern lady, with a passion for sugared tea. "Well, just don't become a jetsetter like your parents. I don't think they've stayed at their house more than a few months at a time in the past twenty years. I don't believe I'll ever understand the reason your father wanted a career in recruiting. When Jim retired, I figured at least then he would stay in one place."

Taylor tossed her empty bottle in the recycling bin and strolled into her bedroom. Dropping down on the queen-size bed, she slid off her high heels. Even with her grandmother's gentle nature, she often rehashed complaints Taylor grew tired of listening to. In fact, she could just about recite what would come out of her grandmother's mouth next.

As the words rang in her ears, memories surfaced of growing up without her mom and dad close by.

Taylor used to resent her dad working so much. Since growing into an adult, she saw things differently. She now related to her father's passion for the position he once held with the university.

What bothered her more than her dad's absence was her mother's. She *chose* to accompany her father every time he visited distant schools, leaving Taylor with her grandparents.

Thinking back, she mentally recounted the different states her father represented in his recruiting position. Now it wasn't work keeping her parents away. It was friends and past connections. Taylor had resigned herself to the facts—they didn't plan on changing. Traveling was their way of life. She accepted that. Granny didn't.

"When I get tired of my career, then I'll consider settling down. If I do have kids one day, I promise I will be there for them."

Taylor sat on the bed and scrunched her toes in the white carpet while she waited for a response. "Well, enough about my son. Since you're not moving in with me, I've decided to stay here at Louise's house. We can help each other in our older years. Her quarters are all on one floor, so there are no steps for me to trip on. Since she's a widow too, there's plenty of room."

Taylor smiled to herself, glad the conversation shifted. "I want you to be happy. I'll support your decision. Do you need me to pack your personal things?"

KAY HARRISON HELD the phone to her ear and grinned, her heart beating in anticipation and lifting her emotions like a flowing fountain. Of all the possibilities ahead, hopefully she could manage to help her granddaughter see life a little differently.

She rested on a decorative pillow as she sat in a black suede lounger. Kay pressed the lever to the chair and straightened the seat as she filled in her granddaughter on her plans to upgrade and prepare the house for sale. "I need you to send the things I want over here to Louise's place. There is a lot of furniture and bric-a-brac to be carted off to the homeless shelter or a thrift shop."

She paused to take a sip of tea.

"Taylor, I also want you to take anything you may want. I've spoken with your father. Jim wants the antique bedroom suite in the end room upstairs, as well as the china cabinet and silver tea set. Those items need to be shipped to your dad's house."

Fearing how her granddaughter would react, Kay rushed the last words. "I'll also need you to supervise the renovations if I'm going to put my home on the market. I want it to be perfect."

"Uh-huh…sure…" Taylor mumbled, then she snapped to attention. "Wait, what? *Supervise?* Granny Kay, I will pack your things and clear out the house, but I don't see any reason I need to oversee the renovations. Why not just list your place for sale as it is? Let the new owners do the work. Some folks love a fixer-up."

Disappointed, Kay placed her tumbler on the glass side table. She adored her granddaughter with all her heart and prayed each day Taylor would realize other things in life were more important than work. Kay's one desire was for her granddaughter to find true happiness—the kind that included fun and other things that existed outside of a job. She also petitioned Jesus each day, asking for Taylor's heart to desire a closer relationship with the Lord. "I wish matters could be handled so easily. I'm afraid my moving out of the home is a bit more complicated." Kay fidgeted with her tumbler. "I can't discuss the situation over the telephone. You need to hear everything in person. Come over Sunday, and we'll have lunch. I will explain things then."

CHAPTER TWO

KAY PLACED THE phone in its cradle and eyed her friend, Louise Matthews. Observing her latest outfit, Kay grinned with fondness. Louise surely owned a jogging suit of every color. Today she wore a new lavender one.

The tinkling sound of a Ten Commandments bracelet jingled in the air as Louise poured them both more tea.

"So do you think you'll convince her?" Louise stepped back, clearly waiting for an answer.

"One way or the other, I have to get Taylor to spend time at the family home. The ring hasn't been found in fifty years. I doubt she'll find my treasure, but I won't rest easy until I convince her to explore all the rooms again." Kay swiped at a wrinkle on her pants. "Who knows? Maybe she can search in places I never looked before. There's always hope. I haven't been in that old attic for a long time. I can't even remember what's up there." Kay shrugged. "The positive side of this is she'll have to use some of her vacation time and slow down a bit. Taylor's been working too hard and needs a break from her job. One day, she will thank me."

SUNDAY AFTERNOON CAME. Yawning, Taylor stood on the porch of Louise's single-story brick house. She rubbed her eyes and squinted, trying to adjust to the bright sunshine. Scanning the yard while she waited for someone to answer the door, she scrutinized the lawn. The grass had recently been mowed and new flowering bushes planted. A birdbath stood to the side of the home, filled with fresh water for all the feathered friends to enjoy.

Louise paid a teenager in the neighborhood to tend to the grounds. As nice as the view was, Taylor wished that instead of standing at the entrance of Louise's quaint abode in Liberty Cove, she was lounging at her condo.

Anyway, she'd been cut a small break. She'd slept in, at least. This was the second Sunday of the month—if it weren't for the broken hip her grandmother suffered, Taylor would have needed to arrive much earlier to attend church. Over the past years, that had become their usual routine.

Taylor shook her head and she couldn't help but smile. Granny Kay always found a reason to get her in church at least once a month. Usually the second Sunday—Donut Sunday—was when her grandmother reminded her of worship services, using pastries as a bribe. Taylor had just accepted it as part of their relationship. A bluebird fluttered in a nest nearby. The movement drew her attention to the little creature. She remembered a childhood story her grandmother told her years earlier which evolved a bird, a king, and how God used a tiny feather to guide the king. As if God asked a question, Taylor spoke out. "Yes, Lord, I do believe in you. I just don't have a lot of spare time. I'm not even sure I'm cut out to be one of those church ladies. My life's too busy. How Granny Kay did it all these years is beyond me."

THE SUN BEAT down on the umbrella shading the table as Taylor picked at her salad, eating small bites. A butterfly's wings fanned back and forth on a nearby black-eyed Susan. The fragile yellow insect dashed in flight and caught her attention.

Taylor looked at her watch and took another glimpse at her grandmother, waiting for her to finish eating so she could find out what could be so important.

Finally, her grandmother laid her fork to rest and focused on the issue at hand—the supposed need for Taylor to oversee renovations at the Harrison family estate. "You know, it might be fun for you to take a little vacation and stay in one of the bedrooms before it's sold. That way, you can make sure the work is done to satisfaction."

"I just don't think I can. I'm sorry."

Granny Kay placed her fork at the side of her plate and wiped her mouth with a napkin. "I realize you don't understand why this means so much to me, but it does. The house has been in the family a long time. When I sell the place, I want it perfect." She threw down her paper towel and in a voice uncharacteristic of her slow southern drawl, she spilled the rest of her words. "And sweetheart...I also need you to find my ring before the home is sold."

"What ring?"

"You know that generations of our relatives have owned the place. Your great-grandmother relocated to smaller quarters after she was widowed, and she gave the dwelling to my brother, Paul, and his new bride." Kay's voice cracked. "They moved in right after their honeymoon. My brother was so happy. He couldn't wait to start a family and fill the rooms with lots of children."

"Oh yes." Taylor swallowed a sip of tea. "I remember you talking about him to Louise when I was a young girl. You said something about him and his wife getting shot."

Kay closed her eyes and shook her head in agreement. "Such an unhappy time. They weren't even married a year before someone broke into the house and killed both of them. I found out later that when Paul transferred the deed into his and Elizabeth's names, he also drew up a will adding me as his second beneficiary."

"And this ring you spoke of?"

Kay took a drink from her glass and shivered. "Elizabeth had a beautiful square sapphire ring my mother gave her. It was a family treasure that'd been handed down for generations. Back then, I had just graduated high school, and the tradition in our household was to give the ring to the first one to marry. On the day of Elizabeth and Paul's wedding, she told me she was going to pass the ring on to me when I married. She was a lovely dear."

"But she died before that could happen." Taylor added her piece to the puzzle.

"Correct. The police wouldn't let me into the house until four months after they were shot. I searched every room." Kay took a heavy breath. "I never found the ring. A year later, I married your grandfather. We remodeled most of the rooms and spent years filling the spaces with good memories. My only regret is that I couldn't have any more children after I had Jim."

"That's quite a story." Never had Taylor thought much about the conversation she'd walked in on when she was twelve. Now, though, many unanswered thoughts ran through her mind. Pushing aside her half-empty tumbler of tea, she raised her brows at the question in the forefront of her mind. "How could you live in that house, knowing such a horrible thing happened there?"

The question lit up Kay's face. "I've never wanted to live anywhere else. Even though the circumstances were terrible, they never took away the love inhabiting those rooms. If you have enough faith, the good will always outshine the bad. Sometimes you must believe in your heart."

"It's a good thing I never knew as a kid. I would have had nightmares."

"You adored your home. I did too. Unfortunately, I can no longer take care of the big place. My legs won't let me go up and down those steps anymore. I can't stand the thought of leasing the place out. I've heard stories from my friends about how complicated matters can become when you rent. I'm too old for the hassle and I don't want to leave it empty either. You don't want it, so that leaves me with one choice: sell. Maybe a couple will buy the house and fill the rooms with family again. That's why it's important for you to be there when the work is done. Dear, the house is more than a bunch of boards. It's part of our family. I don't mind letting it go if I have to. I just want people to see the wonderful possibilities inside those walls. My old family home is special to me." Kay took a sip of her beverage. "Not only do I want to modernize the residence so younger families can enjoy it the way I have, I also can't be satisfied until I'm certain all those rooms have been combed through and searched one more time. I imagine the ring is there somewhere."

"Does the ring mean that much, Granny?"

"The sapphire came from our descendants, and as a child, I always dreamed of wearing it and one day passing it on. Did you know that sapphires are a prominent stone in the Bible—a symbol of joyful devotion to God? There have never been any secrets concerning my ancestors' faith in the Lord. It's the same trust I carry with me each day." Smiling, she continued. "Oh yes, it does mean a lot to me. It would be wonderful to recover the ring. I've shuffled around the place off and on for years and haven't found it. That haunts me. With the rooms empty and the renovations being done, you might just be able to rummage around and find different spots to examine. Think of it as my last wish before I die."

Taylor's mouth opened, ready to blurt out all the reasons she couldn't do this. She didn't have time. She didn't want to take off work—until those last words her grandmother said jumped into her head and settled in her heart. A knife slicing through her chest couldn't have hurt worse. "You don't talk like that. You have a lot of life to live."

Kay lifted her head toward Taylor and waved her hand in the air. "Oh poo, I'm not saying I'm dying right now. But I would love to see the family heirloom again. Once the house is sold, so are my chances."

Lowering her voice, the older woman pushed back a lock of her short ringlets. Her eyes focused on Taylor and her voice quivered as she made her last plea. "I don't have anyone else to ask. Your dad told me a while back he didn't have time for such nonsense. I don't think he even believes the story. But I know it's true. I remember how the stone shined. That piece of jewelry was beautiful. Elizabeth meant to give it to me. I don't want our generation to be the dead end."

Taylor stared at her grandmother and witnessed a surge of pain from the long-ago trauma now visible in the older lady's eyes.

Motionless, she sat in her chair. How could she help her grandmother and still concentrate on her job?

As she scooted out of her seat, Taylor's thoughts ran amuck with the story of the murder and the tale of a missing gemstone.

"The killer probably stole the ring when he broke into the house. I imagine it's long gone by now."

Granny moved to the edge of her chair. "No, the ring has to be misplaced somewhere in one of the rooms. The police caught the man a year later."

She then extended her hand in a motion meant for Taylor to help her to her feet. "My brother was an accountant, and this man was a client of Paul's. The guy lost all his capital because of a bad stock purchase he insisted my brother make for him. In the end, he blamed Paul when he lost his money. Their deaths were some kind of twisted revenge."

"That's awful."

"The authorities questioned him about the jewelry. The man swore he didn't know anything about any personal items, and nothing else was missing."

"But he may have lied. He still could have stolen the ring. Maybe he hid it or sold it."

"No. About a year later, he wrote to me and apologized for his terrible actions. While in prison, he turned his life over to Jesus. I wrote back and asked him about the ring. He didn't take it. It's in that house, I'm certain. Taylor, please think about what I said. You haven't taken a vacation since you became a CEO at Mugful's."

Taylor sighed. "Well..."

"Perhaps you could take a few weeks off. I have a carpenter scheduled to come by next week. We're going to go over plans to turn one of the upstairs bedrooms into a library and tear down a few walls on the main floor to create an open-concept living-dining area." With a deep breath, Kay looked across the yard and back at her granddaughter. "The house is traditional and from a time period a lot of people admire. But back then rooms were chopped up. All the ladies at church tell me that the big fascination nowadays is an unrestricted flow between the main living areas. I'm ashamed to admit most of the rooms still have pea-green floor covering. Long ago, when it was installed, carpet was all the rage and green was a popular color. I never replaced the rugs. Hardwood is the style today."

Taylor barely listened as she paced the sundeck and came to a halt in front of her grandmother. She hugged herself while pushing her lips together. Taylor breathed in a lungful of air. "You're asking a lot of me. I need to think about this."

AN HOUR LATER, Taylor headed down the road toward the interstate, her emotions pulling her in many directions. Before she took the exit to the super highway, she pulled into the local Grab-N-Go Convenience Mart. The turmoil churning in her mind had her stomach rolling like a beach ball.

A Coke and a bottle of aspirin were foremost on her mind. How could she fulfill her grandmother's wish? Taylor had worked hard to build a good reputation at Mugful's. Everyone in the office counted on her. No, that wasn't the problem—she didn't *want* to take time off, even though she'd saved all her vacation hours for the past two years.

Taylor drove the miles toward Raleigh. Even the budding trees and greenery of the new season didn't make the decision remaining before her go away. All the talk about family today brought a few childhood memories to her mind.

Liberty Cove Junior High popped in her memory. Many times she'd wished her parents would have delayed a trip or an event to come to her ballet recital or a school function.

As she exited off the interstate, she admonished herself for dwelling on the past again. Then it came to her. During those years of growing up, sometimes she felt like a ship's rudder, tossed to and fro, never knowing when her parents would be around to show their daughter support. She'd felt abandoned, sometimes even unwanted.

Taylor's brow furrowed, and her throat stung as pangs tussled in her conscience. On too many occasions she'd looked out into the audience and seen empty seats where her parents should have been.

But Granny Kay was always there.

The past had molded her, driven her to put everything she had into a career. Her job was the one thing she had control over. As long as she did her best, she could count on it to be there. It was a root of her life, her reason for being who she was.

But her grandmother was another foundation she leaned on. Could she do to her grandmother what her parents had done to her all those years?

Taylor entered the city and turned onto the street to her apartment, and her point of view shifted. No matter what project she had been involved with when she was young, her grandmother supported her. She taught Taylor that family was something you should hold onto, regardless of how difficult things seemed.

The sacrifices her grandparents had made through the years had instilled in Taylor a concrete principle: sometimes a person should do things for others, particularly loved ones, even if their plans were interrupted. Simply because it was the right thing.

As she turned into her driveway, a scripture ran through her mind. The verse was one she remembered her grandmother quoting. She didn't recall the stanza's exact wording, but it said something about doing for others with a good heart, the same way you would for God. *Man, Granny Kay, you have a way of getting to me—even an hour's drive away.*

CHAPTER THREE

THE FOLLOWING FRIDAY, Taylor glanced around her office. The desk was cleared of the usual files. Silence filled the room where the hum of the computer was usually heard. Earlier in the week, she had spoken to her boss, Mr. Zimmerman. He assured her things were on a steady flow for now, and since her vacation time had accumulated, it was hers for the taking.

Taylor guaranteed her boss she would be reachable if he needed her and offered to check in at the office once a week. Earlier, she had set up remote connections to her laptop, making it possible to have access to any of her office files, no matter where she was. The phone sounded in the quiet room.

"Taylor, you almost ready to come to Liberty Cove?"

"Yes, Granny Kay. I'm just gathering a few files I'll need. I'll be there in the morning."

"Good, stop by Louise's and we will have breakfast before you go to my house."

"Okay, I should be there by nine"

She pulled the door closed behind her and walked toward the exit of her corporate world. Why did this have to happen now? The last thing she wanted was to waste her vacation time hanging around and watching some man revolutionize her grandmother's house. If she had to take the days, she'd much rather spend them on the beach somewhere. She and Granny could even enjoy a cruise.

But deep down, Taylor acknowledged she'd probably never take the time for those things either.

Granny Kay felt this was important, and she'd honor that. *If it was me, I'd just sell the place and get it over with...unless this ring of hers is worth a lot of money.*

THE NEXT MORNING, Taylor sat at the kitchen table across from her grandmother. "Granny Kay, before I start sorting through your things, have you decided what you want me to do with it? You know there's ten rooms of furniture and trinkets to pack."

"Yes, I know. And I wish I had the strength to help more, but I just haven't been myself lately, since I fell. I did go over to my house last week. Louise helped me sort through the important stuff, and I hired a small moving van. Those guys were good at loading what I told them to carry away. I put some things in a storage unit for now. Taylor, you know how people accumulate junk and outdated electronics. The main things I aim to keep I've gathered. The rest of the contents in the house must go to a re-sale store. The leftovers inside should be discarded. " Granny Kay reached across the table, laying her hand on top of Taylor's.

"Hun, take what you will from our family home. Your dad gave me a short list of things he wanted to keep, so the rest needs to be tossed out or recycled. Whatever you decide is fine with me. As I said, I have all I want to hang on to."

HER LUXURY COMPACT turned onto Alder Court. Taylor parked in the circle drive in front of the massive two-story Victorian. Stepping out of the car, she adjusted her sunglasses and scanned the facade of the house. Despite being dated on the inside, the place was immaculate on the outside. The white house glistened from the spotless sheen of recent paint, keeping the century-old charm intact. Two huge columns stood mounted on each side of the wide cement steps. The gables drew attention to the unique shingles. A few ivy vines extended upward to a bedroom window.

Taylor grabbed her suitcase from the vehicle and beheld the trellis of running roses at the garage, taking one last look at the outside. It was a structure that still retained time-honored allure with just enough present-day touches to please the eye.

Over the years, her grandmother had spent many hours outside in the summer, keeping the flowers and greenery. Taylor recalled one particular conversation in which she'd tried to convince Grandma to pay the yard-mowing man to tend the flowers too. Her grandmother only smiled from under the brim of her sunhat and told her she enjoyed taking care of the plants and watching them flourish. It kept her young.

Taylor's gaze moved to the end of the house. The balcony outside her grandmother's bedroom caught her attention. She smiled, noticing the oval roof over the terrace. Taylor remembered she used to love standing there, looking out at the lawn.

Slowly, she ambled up the flight of stairs and stood between the extra-large pillars. She caught sight of the wooden swing, and she couldn't help picturing herself and Granny Kay in it, moving back and forth. She'd spent many nights there, confiding in her grandmother about boys, friendships, and worries.

Shaking loose the memories, she carried her suitcase to the guest quarters located off the kitchen. Taylor planned on staying there instead of upstairs. The room, although it was smaller than the others, was one of her favorites and provided easy access to the eat-in kitchen and the espresso machine she brought with her.

Taylor planned on working on her laptop at the small kitchen table. No way was she letting this little project of her grandmother's mess up the years of hard work she had put in. After all, besides her grandmother, her career was all she had. She loved her parents, but their weekly phone calls from various hotels or resorts didn't count for a lot.

Taylor busied herself with unpacking, grateful her grandfather had updated this bedroom before he died, installing an enclosed shower in the attached bath and replacing the carpet. She stepped into the kitchen located beside the guest room entryway and placed her two-cup stand, meant to hold her favorite mugs, along with her beverage machine on the speckled countertop. As far as she was concerned, the small appliance was a must have. Then she rummaged around in the kitchen. The huge wooden cabinets were still gray, the color her grandparents painted them six years ago, in an attempt to match the tone on the work surface.

Opening and closing the doors overwhelmed her. Indeed, cleaning out this big house and searching for a tiny ring was going to be an enormous undertaking.

Since her grandmother couldn't tell her where the ring might have been lost, she planned to begin in the kitchen and then search every room as she emptied it. Taylor harbored doubts of finding anything after all these years. Still, there was much to be done to get her grandmother's things packed and shipped. She may as well make the best of her time and use every opportunity to search any obscure areas otherwise easily missed.

Taylor stood in the cooking area, wondering why she didn't explore all these rooms when she was little. She might have found it then. As a child, she never scouted out closets or the attic the way most did. She'd been more of the doll type back then.

Yes, she had lots to do with packing and clearing out all the items and examining all the crooks and crannies an old house held. After all, she believed in doing everything to the best of one's ability.

THE NEXT DAY, she called her grandmother. "Hi, Granny Kay."

"Taylor, how are you this morning? I hope you're not dreading the packing too much."

"Granny Kay, I admit this isn't something I want to do, but for you I will. Someone has to pack the house up and considering your missing ring, it needs to be me, I suppose."

"You're a wonderful granddaughter. I'm so grateful to you, dear."

After her conversation, she spread cardboard boxes across the kitchen floor and filled them with dishes and pots from the cabinets. She left only a few essentials in the first cupboard.

Lowering herself, she squatted on her knees to look below the sink. With childlike curiosity, she eyed the cabinets under the countertop, peering into the dark space. Since the house was longstanding, the cavity was lengthy and narrow. Due to the odd measurements, her grandmother had stopped using the space years ago. All that remained were a few plastic bowls that needed to be thrown away.

Taylor retrieved a small flashlight from a cabinet drawer, positioned herself inside the opening, and crawled a few feet toward the farthest end, peeking for any lose boards or cracks.

Heavy footsteps flooded the room. Taylor's body jerked at the unexpected sound. The reaction sent her head into a metal pipe, giving the top of her skull a hard whack. Stars floated across her vision as she rubbed her head. A loud protest escaped from her lips. As quickly as she could, she crawled back out of the tight hole and whirled around to stand.

A tall, muscular man leaned against the table. "Problems, miss?"

Taylor shot the guy an angry glare as she gave him a quick once-over, noticing his jean-clad legs were crossed at the ankles.

Feeling the heat rise to her cheeks, Taylor met the smug, cocky grin on his face. Even with the shock of finding a stranger in the house, tugs of curiosity seeped from deep within her soul. A little voice inside her head demanded to be heard, announcing the arrival of one of the handsomest men she had seen in a while.

A dimpled chin. Dark blond hair. Defined muscles. In spite of her anger at him for appearing in her house uninvited, the word hottie stampeded her mind.

No, she wasn't going to fall for looks—lots of men were attractive. Most times, they were also conceited, and he certainly radiated the attitude. "Who are you? Why are you in my kitchen?"

AMUSED, BRENT ROBERTS stared at the woman before him with her hands on her hips. In spite of her tousled ringlets scattered askew her head, she was a classy, tall female with wide, captivating eyes.

A chuckle rumbled in his chest at the tone of superiority in her voice. "I'm the contractor Kay Harrison hired to renovate this house. I let myself in with the key she gave me."

Taylor narrowed her eyes. Silently, she scolded her grandmother for giving a key to someone she didn't know. With no intention of exchanging pleasantries, she extended her hand and spoke in a harsh tone. "I'm Taylor Harrison, her granddaughter, and I'm staying here. There is no need for you to have a key."

He shrugged in a nonchalant manner and held out the key. "Name's Brent Roberts. Kay Harrison said you might stay here to pack her belongings and answer any questions that may come up with while remodeling."

TAYLOR GLARED AT the man. His self-assured posture as he leaned against the table irritated her more than she wanted to admit.

"Well, Mr. Roberts, I trust you won't need to rely heavily on my input. Since my grandmother hired you, I'll assume you're competent and aware of what she wants accomplished around here. Be assured I'll be watching to make sure paid time isn't squandered or materials wasted. Meanwhile, this house needs to be cleared out and my grandmother's belongings moved." Taylor snagged the key to the front door and tucked it in her pocket. "Hence, the reason I'm here."

"Sure thing." With a smirk—as if he were patronizing her—Brent turned, strolling out of the kitchen. Before he left, he glanced back and flashed a smile, revealing a set of pearly whites. "Okay, Ms. Harrison. I'll be here at seven in the morning. You can let me in, and if you have any coffee made, I might drink a cup before my crew arrives."

Taylor's eyes widened in disbelief, and she marched after him. "How dare you assume I'm going to cater to you, Mr. Roberts?" She walked briskly to the front entrance, only to find him gone. He'd left plans for the overhaul of several rooms lying rolled up on an antique desk beside the entry.

Already she didn't care for him! Some relaxing vacation this would be.

Taylor rubbed her arms and stomped back into the kitchen. This was going to the longest few weeks she'd ever experienced.

THE SUN SHINED through the lace curtains hanging in the guest room. Taylor woke to the sound of the door chimes clanging throughout the house. "It's too early!" she complained, groaning. Sitting up in bed, she rubbed her face, and reality hit. It must be seven o'clock. Taylor gritted her teeth and tossed the comforter off her body.

On her way out of the room, she grabbed her purple robe and slipped it on, complaining to herself, "The most big-headed contractor around." *The day hasn't even started, and I have to deal with the likes of him.*

Brent waited, fingers tapping impatiently on the frame, as she swung the door open. His vision boldly traveled the length of her legs and lingered on the clumsy tie holding her satin robe together.

Taylor bit her lower lip. *The gall of this man!*

Quickly, she chastised herself. *Tomorrow morning I will be up and dressed before he arrives.*

"Well, I see you're on time. I'll dress and leave you to your plans."

Brent tossed his head sideways. He made an exaggerated point of looking her body up and down once more. "Don't hurry on my account." He stifled a grin. "I've always found silk appealing on a lady, and you wear it very well, Ms. Harrison."

Taylor's pulse raced. Her mouth flew open to speak.

The thought of her grandmother stopped her. The words she wanted to express—about the kind of man she believed him to be—would wait. She needed to put on some clothes.

If only she could tell him to leave and never come back. Determined to convince her grandmother to hire someone else, she whirled around and trudged toward the guest room.

FORTY-FIVE MINUTES later, Taylor breezed into the kitchen. With loathing, she eyed a jar of instant coffee that sat on the back of the sink. *Disgusting.* Her lips curled as she prepared her special espresso. How anyone consumed that jarred caffeinated garbage was a puzzle. Anyway, it didn't matter. That vain man could drink mud for all she cared. He deserved burnt grounds instead of a coffee with real taste.

Taylor worked on her laptop until lunch time. Then she closed her computer and concentrated on packing the kitchen. One more trip to the local Salvation Army and this room would be clean, except for the appliances and small round table at the end wall close to the guest room. All the searching she had done so far proved hopeless. The chances of finding anything other than the gold-colored napkin holder, lost years ago, were slim.

She pitched it on the table and turned, observing the cabinets. The only place left to look was on top of those cupboards. Her plan when she returned. A step stool was in the pantry. She could use the extra height to reach on top of the cabinets. Maybe someone had been hidden the ring there for safekeeping.

TAYLOR STOOD OVER the sink, using a rag to swab the very top of the tall cabinet. Carefully, she held onto the cupboard handle and made her way past the basin along the narrow work surface.

A noise startled her, making her miscalculate the width of the area. Taylor's foot missed the edge. She slipped and fell.

Unexpected arms caught her in midair. "Ms. Harrison, you need to be careful. You'll get hurt."

Taylor was stunned by the brawny arms that caught her; by the easy, efficient way he seemed to swoop her to safety when she should have landed hard on her bottom.

For a second, she froze, unable to stop her eyes from following an imaginary path down his cheek, leading to his lips, then continuing to the dimple in his chin. For one split-second, her body responded to the pressure of his chest. She scrunched her face, determined to ignore the feeling caused by the close contact. "Mr. Roberts, put me down. I'm fine."

With a sideways smile, he positioned her feet on the floor. "Considering I've held you in my arms now, you should call me Brent."

Taylor straightened her t-shirt and glanced away from the mischievous glint his eyes held. Against her resolve, she heard her voice say, "I'm Taylor."

FOR THE NEXT hour, Taylor sat at the table with Brent, and he showed her the designs for remodeling. He detailed plans to tear down walls to open up the main areas. He also gave her a tentative schedule of hours he and his workers would be present at the house. Brent then asked what arrangements she'd made for clearing out the living room so they could start knocking down walls to open the sections.

Every so often, Brent would look up from his blueprint and flash his crooked grin. Taylor tried her best to show only a professional interest. She just couldn't shake the shiver of excitement or stop emotions from creeping through her every time she remembered being in his arms. Even though they were from two different worlds, and he seemed to think himself superior, she couldn't help being attracted to him, a feeling that warmed her to her toes.

She glanced sideways at him, noticing his outdoor tan and broad shoulders. In spite of her determination to ignore Brent, Taylor couldn't stop herself from comparing him to some blue-collar guy you would see on a billboard. Somehow, even his cocky grin made him appealing. *Humph! If you like that sort of man!*

Of course, she didn't. Not at all...

THREE DAYS LATER, Taylor woke earlier than usual. Her previous concern about managing much rest while staying here, especially after hearing the story her grandmother had told her, vanished.

Granny Kay was right. Even though the house was large and had a checkered past, there was a tranquil serenity here. It was home. She slept like a baby, just the way she did at her condo.

Taylor sat at the kitchen table, working on the reports for Mugful's. Her phone sounded, playing the usual coastal music theme. She saved her file on her laptop and picked up her cell.

Her grandmother's voice sang out in a happy tone. "Taylor, how are things going?"

"Good. I cleared most of the junk out of the kitchen. I haven't had any luck finding the ring yet. There are a lot of rooms to check out and piles of things to move." Taylor rose from her seat and refilled her mug.

"Well, at least you are looking, Taylor. I can't tell you what this means to your old granny."

Taylor chuckled. "Don't use that apologetic tone with me. I know you can't search for anything right now. I'm your granddaughter. It's my job to help if I can."

"Well, I want you to know what it means to me. Please, if there's anything I can do to make your job easier, let me know."

"Well, one thing bothers me—your choice of contractors. Granny Kay, he's an egotistical, obnoxious smart-aleck. Thinks way too much of himself."

"Taylor, obviously he came highly recommended. Brent and his crew do a great job turning old houses into modern dwellings. He's also an honest man. I don't want you to be uncomfortable, but give him a chance...you'll see."

So much for "anything you need."

Taylor sighed then closed her eyes for a second. "Okay, I'll try. After all, it's just for a few weeks. Then this house will be finished, and you can sell it."

Her grandmother gave her some encouragement concerning the search for the ring and then said goodbye. Taylor opened her file again, determined to finish her report before the noisy banging of repairs began.

LOUISE STARED ACROSS the room at her lifelong friend. "Kay, what did she say?"

Kay leaned back in her seat and tossed a satisfied squint in her friend's direction. "She hasn't found the ring, and she thinks Brent is several unpleasant things—one of them being a smart-aleck."

Louise rose to gather the coffee cups from the table, shaking her head. "What, my nephew? No way. That boy has always been a gentleman."

"Seems they rub each other the wrong way. I think it's good for Taylor to be around a man who's not a wimp. Louise, we just need to pray more about her situation. You and I know God will work everything out if we believe and trust in His word. Taylor needs to see life should revolve around more than her career. It's good for her to take a break from her office. I'm thinking Brent may be another helpful aspect. The last man Taylor was involved with seemed to think only of things he wanted. We both know Brent is anything but selfish. Taylor can't see past the last relationship. Who knows? Maybe spending time with your nephew is just what the doctor ordered."

TAYLOR CLOSED HER laptop as the sound of footsteps echoed from the foyer. Taking a long breath, she shook her head. Her peace was gone. Brent and the work crew had arrived. She may as well start her daily chore of packing and hunting for Granny Kay's ring.

"Good morning. I brought you a muffin from the local bakery."

"You did?" Taylor plugged her computer into the wall socket to charge and suspiciously eyed the white bag Brent held out.

"Sure. Hope you like blueberry."

"Uh...thanks." She was at a loss. *Why would he bring me a muffin?* Atomically, she reached inside to grab hold of the offering. *May as well eat it.*

Uncertain how to respond to his kind demeanor, she offered the only thing she could think of. "I have coffee made, if you would like a cup."

"Sure. Thanks." Brent walked over to the cabinet and took out his cup, perched beside a jar of instant he had placed in the space the day before.

As he reached for the decanter, he noticed Taylor's stein holder. "What's the gold lettering say on your cups?" He didn't wait for Taylor to answer but came back with his own response. "Mugful's—that's an espresso coffee place in Raleigh. Is that where you work?"

"I do."

Brent considered her thoughtfully. Something about her told him there was more to Taylor Harrison than the hard-headed woman she appeared to be. Underneath her independent non-nonsense shell, he sensed something different. For reasons he didn't quite understand, he stopped asking about her job.

"Taylor, if you need any help moving the furniture, my guys can lend a hand."

Taylor stopped chewing and eyeballed Brent. What was his deal? She decided he was only trying to be helpful. "No, thanks. I have a truck coming the day after tomorrow to haul away the furniture. I plan to keep a few antiques, so the movers will take them to my condo. Over the weekend, I should clear out most of the items downstairs."

She looked up from her blueberry muffin as Brent sat at the table across from her. He took a sip of her special brew, and shock registered on his face. He pointed to his cup and held his hand on his throat. He shook his head in an attempt to say something that wouldn't come out.

Taylor couldn't hold back the laughter. She chuckled at his show of intense dislike. "So, Mister Big-shot, not used to espressos, huh? It's time you were brought up to speed into the real world.

That coffee you are drinking is one of the finest gourmet blends around."

"Awful. No, thanks." Brent coughed, wobbling his head back and forth as if attempting to protest. He stalked to the sink and poured the contents of his cup down the drain, reaching for his jar of roasted coffee. "Taylor, I'm sorry. My caffeine preferences are limited. I know you work for Mugful's, but I like regular java. Maybe a cappuccino once in a while. That's about the extent of my coffee likes."

Brent spooned the dark grounds into his cup, running the tap water to get it hot. "Listen, I'll need you to go with me to pick new flooring."

Despite the humor of the coffee situation, Taylor's mood sobered. The last thing on her to-do list was going somewhere with this man. Taylor quickly glanced over at Brent. It was all she could do not to stare into those baby-blues. A fleeting thought passed through her mind. The color of his eyes reminded her of a summer sky on a cloudless day.

Shaking the notion away, she waved her hand in the air, dismissing the idea. "I don't need to accompany you. You pick out whatever you like. It doesn't matter to me."

"Taylor, I don't know how things are done in Raleigh, but here I cater to my clients' wishes. It is your grandmother's request that I include you in all my decisions. Usually I take samples to the owners and everything is tabulated on the invoice. However, Mrs. Harrison specifically asked me to get your approval on all the purchases."

Taylor rose and walked over to the sink. "I'll have a talk to my grandmother about that." While she spoke, she dialed Granny Kay's number. Tapping her foot, she counted the rings until the away message broke into the ring tone.

Brent watched her eyes narrow as she ended the call. "Taylor, that's fine if you can get the okay from her, but for now I have a schedule to keep." Brent turned and his arm touched her shoulder, then he slid his hand onto hers. The warmth of his touch moved over her body. His eyes searched her face, probing into her soul. "I promise I'll be good company."

Taylor jerked her hand away as if she touched the top of a hot stove. She rushed to the other side of the room. Keeping her back to him, she spoke in haste. "If I must. Just let me know when you're ready, and I'll follow you in my car."

EVENING CAME, BRENT and the small crew left, and Taylor set out to survey sections of the rooms downstairs. Rubble from the facelift in progress was scattered around, and she stepped over remains to reach to the rooms at the back of the house.

They had been cleared earlier in the day, and now she could search the empty partitions. Taylor walked the perimeter of a portion that used to be her grandfather's study. When she finished poking around in the closet, she ran her hand around a wide window frame, feeling for anything.

A shiny object caught her attention under the sill. Something lay in a crack, stuck between the floor and the wide molding that ran the length of the wall. Taylor stooped down and wriggled at the item until she wrested the piece loose.

One look at the relic made her sit hard on the floor. Recollections flooded, taking her back to a time when she was a little girl. Her grandfather was working at his desk, and she was playing on the floor with her dolls. That day, he had joked with her about the outfit she had chosen for the figurine to wear. Taylor held tight to the old plastic circle that was once a beautiful silver crown for her Barbie. As she relived that day, a tear slipped down her check. Memories. It was just like that old saying—they sure were bittersweet.

THE NEXT WEEK, Taylor divided her time between her work duties and exploring the house for the ring. She had gotten into a habit of traveling to Raleigh on Wednesdays to make sure everything at Mugful's was on a regular schedule.

The search for her grandmother's treasure had her seeing the house in a new light. She'd spent a lot of time in this residence as a kid, seeing it through the eyes of a child. Now though, she discovered a different appreciation for her surroundings. Somehow, the old dwelling didn't seem as formidable as it once had.

As she gathered and packed things, she came to understand why her grandmother loved the house so much. The ceilings were high, and each room was adorned with wide molding that ran the length of the walls. Unique edging framed out the corners, ornamented with decorative sconces that hugged the topmost part of the wall. Yes, her ancestors' home was indeed a luxury anyone would appreciate. She might even enjoy it herself—*if* she were ready to settle down and start a family. This was the kind of a place that needed children's laughter filling it.

Taylor concentrated on removing all her grandparents' belongings from the remaining rooms downstairs. She figured she would leave the guest quarters, where she was staying, until very last. As the hours whittled away, she explored closets and open spaces, any areas a precious stone could hide. Every once in a while, she was slammed with memories from the past.

In the formal living room, once the carpet was stripped from the floor, she found a childhood bracelet stuck in a loose board in the closet. Biting her bottom lip, Taylor smiled. She held the little trinket up to the light and ogled the figurines that hung down. This was a gift that her mom had given her from one of their trips—an apology for missing the school talent show. She could still picture herself opening the pretty red box and pulling out the wristlet.

Another time, she stumbled upon a girl's old makeup kit. Taylor pulled off the plastic cap to reveal the gooey pink substance that used to be lipstick. She turned the tube around in her hand and remembered dressing up and having tea with her grandmother.

Taylor pushed her hair out of her face. All these objects were fun to find and reminisce over. They weren't what she needed to find, though. With each passing day, she had to admit her grandmother's ring seemed lost forever, even with her luck of discovering things from the past. Taylor couldn't help but wonder what possessed her grandmother to believe her treasure was somewhere in this house. Her grandparents had never come upon anything in all the years they lived here. The odds of her finding the heirloom were slim indeed.

THE NEXT DAY, Taylor was up with the sun for reasons unknown to her—she seemed to enjoy rising a little earlier in this house. Once again she set out searching, this time in the main bathroom downstairs. Other than the usual muck and grime, she didn't locate anything worth keeping.

Brent had taken on the habit of bringing her a muffin or biscuit every morning, and in return, they shared a caffeinated beverage before he started his day.

Taylor tried him on a more traditional kind of connoisseur coffee. Knowing her coffee mixtures as well as she did, she picked a café Americano that was a weaker combination. This way he would learn to appreciate a truly good-tasting drink and maybe give up spooning granules into a cup.

Often, he found reasons to hunt her down and talk, touching her in the process. Taylor didn't like to admit it to herself, but she also sought him for conversation. Taylor tried to ignore the sensation of giddiness she experienced when he was near. Despite first impressions, she was slowly seeing him in a different light.

Every time his body bumped against hers, intrigue settled over her. Unable to help herself, she found a way to bump back.

Taylor rolled her eyes at the realization of the little cat-and-mouse game they played together each day. But it was only harmless flirting, right? It wasn't as if he was truly interested in her, or she in him. They were wrong for each other.

CHAPTER FOUR

BRENT ARRIVED AT his usual time with a morning biscuit for Taylor. After their regular breakfast routine, he headed into the space that was looking more like an open living-dining area. Taylor overheard him announce to a guy he called Hank that he would be back in a few hours—he was leaving to purchase the flooring, granite, and pot lighting.

Walking back into the kitchen, Brent asked Taylor if she was ready to pick out some materials for the upgrades. "Yes, I can go. Let me get my keys. I'll follow you in my car."

An odd expression crossed Brent's face. "Why don't you ride with me in my work truck? No sense in wasting gas. That way, we can talk about the plans, and you can give me some more insight on your grandmother's decorating taste."

"Well…" Taylor hesitated and looked down at the floor while she considered his words. Struggling, she searched to find an excuse—any reason at all to say no. Surely she could come up with something.

Those little accidental touches could easily turn into something else. That playful smile of his, and the way he gazed into her eyes…as if he was searching her soul…did he realize how he made her long for something more?

Although he was great eye candy, he wasn't her type. Even with all the mental objections flying around her head, she smiled back and nodded. "Okay, sure."

BRENT HELPED TAYLOR with the high step into his truck. The white, monstrous, four-door vehicle seemed to swallow her up. The side was painted with a flamboyant "Roberts Construction" logo. Funny, she had never noticed his automobile before. Even though he said this was a work truck, a vehicle this expensive wasn't something a typical struggling carpenter would drive, not even for show.

Brent maneuvered the pick-up onto the street toward town. "So, what do you do at that yuppie coffee shop?"

Torn between agitation and amusement, she glanced at him.

"Yuppie?" She laughed. "I haven't heard anyone use that label in a long time. To answer your question, my office is in the corporate building. I'm the executive officer over the southern branches." She gauged his reaction, wondering what he was thinking as his jaw wiggled and the muscles tightened around his face.

When he didn't comment, she continued. "Now it's my turn. How long have you been a contractor?"

He inhaled, as if explaining was going to be a major task. "I worked my summers for my uncle, and then I went to college and earned my architectural degree. I've had my own company for about six years. Funny thing is, I enjoy the physical labor more than sitting behind a desk. So between paperwork and bids for new projects, I work with the guys."

"You started a business young, didn't you?"

"Sometimes things happen. At the time, they may not be what we want. I never considered being a contractor, but here I am."

"So your dreams didn't come true?"

"I wouldn't say that. I've realized situations have a way of working out. If we trust in the Lord, He is always there to guide us—no matter what. There's a verse in the Bible that says God works out things for good for those who love him. I believe that. He knew what I needed in my future. When my uncle died, my aunt asked me to take over his construction business, so here I am."

Taylor listened to the easy way he spoke about life and God. Living in the hustle and bustle of Raleigh, she'd forgotten how much the people of Liberty Cove valued their faith. As they drove the few miles to the only hardware store in the area, she paid attention to the things Brent said, realizing that the old adages about judging books by the cover weren't always true. She had labeled him as a self-centered womanizer. By the time he pulled his truck into the parking lot, she was laughing, enjoying his company, and seeing Brent Roberts as a different person. A feeling of ease settled around her, something she hadn't experienced with a man in a long time.

"WELL, YOU HAVE to choose one. I declare all women are alike."

Taylor tossed Brent a questioning glare. "What's that supposed to mean?"

He leaned in closer to Taylor. His cerulean gaze penetrated hers, and his breath fell on her cheek as he responded in a slow, easy manner. "Women complicate things. Just pick a color already—cherry or hazelnut."

"Men are all the same as well. No patience for making an important decision."

"Fair enough."

With a wry smile, Taylor stepped back, burying her emotional reaction as she pointed to the cherry shade.

While the flooring was being loaded, they moved on to choosing granite for the countertops.

With their shopping finished, they headed in the direction of the house. A couple blocks later, he pulled into a mini-mall parking lot.

"Wait! What are you doing?" The question came out a little too loud as she realized he was parking in front of a restaurant.

Brent glanced sideways at her. "I figured you might like something to eat. I know I could use a bite. My biscuit from this morning is long since digested. I also need to see my sister for a minute while we're here, if you don't mind, and her shop is two doors down from Liberty Cove Bar-B-Que."

Suddenly, Taylor felt silly. Why had she reacted so strongly? So over the top?

Only deep inside, she comprehended the reason—she was beginning to enjoy his company just a little too much. She could handle anything...except the strange emotions he stirred. With her tone apologetic, she said, "I wasn't thinking, of course. You caught me off guard. I would like something to eat."

As they walked toward a small dress shop, memories surfaced of the store where Taylor had worked during college. She had always enjoyed the hustle of merchandise sales and had to admit those days she spent in retail held good memories. "Daisy's Boutique is your sister's place?"

"She's owned it as long as I can remember. Daisy is a lot older than me. I was born when Mom was about forty-two."

Brent opened the glass door and followed her inside.

From the first step into the area, she felt comfortable. The interior was decorated in warm, muted tones with colorful banners that draped the walls, advertising the apparel and accessories. Dresses hung on one wall while pants and tops were fitted in the middle of the room.

TAYLOR STROLLED AHEAD of Brent to a stand that held purses and shoulder bags, giving the two siblings time to talk. From the few words she overheard, Taylor assumed they were discussing their mother.

A few minutes later, he called out and motioned for her to join him at the counter. "This is my sister, Daisy." Taylor shook the hand of the well-dressed lady she surmised to be in her late fifties. It didn't take much to assess that this woman loved embellishments with her outfits. Her wrists were lined with an array of bangles in different colors, and rings adorned her fingers. "Hello, it's good to meet you."

The older lady looked Taylor over and smiled her approval.

"So, Brent is redesigning your grandmother's house. I hope he's not being too obnoxious. I'm afraid he's a bit spoiled. The fault belongs to the Roberts clan. He was a change-of-life baby, and we all catered to him."

Taylor glanced over at Brent and for the first time she saw him blush. "Oh, so that explains it."

Without making a comment, he wrinkled his brow, feigning ignorance. The women paid him no attention as they laughed at the joke shared. The two females spent the next ten minutes talking about the perils and pluses of the retail business.

DURING THEIR MEAL, Taylor found herself at ease and sharing stories about her life. She laughed often at Brent and his feeble attempts at telling a joke.

He attempted to mask sadness that showed on his face when he spoke of his mother's recent health condition. She was in a retirement home and having trouble remembering things.

"Where is your dad?"

Brent swallowed a bite of slaw, washing it down with a sip of tea. "He passed away when I was in junior high. My uncle took over, keeping me busy at his construction sites. That was when I developed a passion for building. My family has always been close. I don't know what I'll do when Daisy leaves. Her husband is retiring from his practice, and the two of them bought a home in Cape Hatteras. Even though that's just a few hours away, it's not the same as being able to stop by her dress shop anytime to say hi."

Taylor ignored the tug at her heart that encouraged her to further question Brent about his sister moving. Instead, she asked him a question that had plagued her for weeks. "Brent, tell me why the macho act?"

Brent stopped eating and wrinkled his face. "What? Me?" He laughed. "Macho, I'm not. Why would you say such a thing?"

"Well, when we first met, you were leaning up against the table like you owned the world. Your face was all smug with this I'm-the-greatest-man-on-earth attitude."

"Hey, remember, you weren't exactly sweet to me." He laughed. "You've misunderstood me from the start. I'm not that sort of guy. Sure, I'm used to making decisions and leading projects. Women count on me either to build them a beautiful house or remodel the one they have into their dream home. I always aim to please."

"Okay, maybe my first impression of you was a bit skewed."

Brent flashed a wide smile and laid his hand on top of Taylor's. "Seriously, the only thing I'm overly confident about is the knowledge that God will guide me each day. If I seem sure of myself, it's because I live my life following the teachings of Jesus. If I came across to you as insensitive, I'm sorry. I just don't worry about things the way others do. Life isn't as earth-shattering as you make it out. Not when you know God has a plan for your life."

THAT AFTERNOON, TAYLOR hunched in front of her laptop. So much to do, so little time, and she couldn't concentrate. Her mind drifted to the events of the day. The lunch with Brent had been relaxing. How long it had been since she'd felt so comfortable with a man?

She didn't quite understand Brent's explanation. *Life happens.* Even though she understood God had a plan for His children, she couldn't grasp how that translated into Brent being so self-assured and confident. Didn't he worry? Care what others thought?

Shaking her head, she decided to give him the benefit of the doubt. Maybe she indeed misread him. He was certainly different than any other man she had known, a bit of an odd sort.

Taylor rubbed the bridge of her nose while her mind lingered on Brent and men in general. How were relationships so easy for some women? The few men she had dated—especially the one she'd believed was her soul-mate—turned out to be superficial jerks. *Surely there's a guy out there who doesn't mind a woman having a career and ideas. One who's not afraid to let a woman climb her own corporate ladder.*

If so, I haven't found him. Better to step back and concentrate on my work. That I can control.

In the next room, she heard Brent and the other carpenters finish for the day. Any other time, the banging and sawing would have caused her to cart her work to the small bedroom and shut the door. Today it didn't seem so bothersome. Maybe because she kept hoping Brent would walk by.

FRIDAY EVENING, BRENT helped his crew clean up for the weekend. The sounds of doors slamming and invites to grab carryout and watch the game ricocheted, followed by the roaring of engines, and the men drove off. Brent sauntered into the kitchen as she was putting away the market analysis she was working on. "I know this is short notice, but take pity on a lonely man. Would you go with me to the Pizza Café?"

Lonely? Hadn't she just heard several guys issue him invitations?

As she twisted her mouth in thought, her better judgment gave way to the pangs of hunger crying out in her stomach. "If you're buying."

THE PIZZA RESTAURANT was small, cozy, which was why he chose it. The seating region was decorated in a theme that gave the customers a sense of being in Italy. A picture of the Leaning Tower was painted on one wall, and the image of rolling hills ornamented the opposite side of the restaurant.

The eatery was full of singles and families. Italian music piped out of speakers, playing low in the background and giving the place a romantic atmosphere, even with the diversity of customers.

Brent studied Taylor with curiosity. Since getting to know her, he'd concluded she wasn't as stuck-up or smug as she'd first seemed. He sensed that was a defense mechanism she used to keep people at arm's length. There was a vulnerable side to her that she didn't often show.

"I know this isn't a five-star bistro or anything ritzy. But I thought our date would be more relaxing and personal here. I wanted to take you out, not just for a meal, but so we could get to know each other better."

Taylor dropped her slice of pizza onto her plate. An alarm blared in her head. *Our date?* The urgency to run from the restaurant and all the way back to Raleigh fell over her like a dark shadow. To Taylor, this was grabbing a bite to eat, nothing more. "Brent, you're a nice guy. But I'm very busy with my career. I don't have a lot of time for a relationship, if that's what you mean."

Brent smiled his usual lopsided grin. "I understand your job's important. Who's to say we can't get better acquainted, maybe become friends, go out on occasional dates—that sort of thing? Sometimes we have to take life one day at a time, and then see where it leads."

He took her silence as agreeing. Why did she seem almost scared at the thought of dating him? Was it him...or the idea of a relationship in general? All he knew was he wanted to break down those walls and peel back the many layers to Taylor Harrison.

Taylor picked up her pizza and took a small bite, glad he understood and put no pressure on her. She didn't need the complications dating could bring into her life. She was married to Mugful's. Brent was a nice-looking guy, but the kind that probably wanted commitment—something she couldn't give right now. Maybe never.

During the passing of the next couple hours, they spoke about the facelifts to the house. Brent shared a few funny stories of what it was like to grow up with a sister who was much older than him. He also commented about his other jobs around the area. Finally, he shined the spotlight on her and asked about her career at Mugful's.

"I stay pretty busy. It's a demanding position. I have five retail stores that count on me to keep things running smoothly so they can concentrate on the beverage sales." Taylor paused as the waitress refilled the glasses with tea. "I also handle the advertising for those branches. At times, I have to step in when a manager has a setback or becomes a problem herself. It's typically pretty hard to get away. But I had lots vacation and personal time available. My boss agreed that I should use up some of those lingering hours. These past couple of weeks are as close to a break as I've come in a long time, but the hard work is worth it to build my career." Taylor reached for a breadstick. "I don't mean to pry, but I'm curious. Why aren't you married with a couple of kids?"

Brent scanned the room, his gaze falling on a nearby family with a crying toddler, and then he grinned at Taylor. "I was about to be married once, intended to have it all—house, kids, the whole shebang—after I graduated. I figured Pam wanted the same thing. Soon after I started at the university, she married one of my friends. I guess that made me gun-shy for a while. Now, as I look back on things, I'm glad she cheated on me. Pam was a good woman, but she was shallow. When you're younger, things like that don't seem to matter. She was pretty and popular. I thought my dreams were coming true because I had a real catch. Turns out she wasn't that at all. Since then, I've come to realize how important it is to have woman by my side who has substance and determination." Brent paused and flashed a big grin Taylor's way. "And of course, one who only has eyes for me. It's nice to debate politics with the fairer sex while they're mesmerized by my charm." He chuckled.

"See...that's what I mean. You *are* a little conceited." Taylor couldn't help herself as she burst out in laughter.

BRENT WALKED TAYLOR to the entrance of the Harrison home and waited as she unlocked the door. He eased up to her and wrapped his arms around her. She felt soft, sweet, and pliable in his arms. When she gazed up at him with those big eyes, he saw a change come from the hard-shelled workaholic exterior she presented.

His arms were warm and inviting, and as he held her, the rest of the world faded away. She placed her hand on his chest and felt his heart beating, pumping quick strokes that spoke of the intensity of the moment. There was something wholly intimate about the sensation of his rapid heartbeat, as if it thudded just for her.

As he held her, her worries faded away. She was safe and comfortable, free of pressures. Mugful's was a distant memory.

She was about to speak when his mouth traveled across the base of her throat then captured her lips. The kiss left no question as to the attraction he felt for her.

As their lips met again and heat flooded her, she second-guessed the last few hours. Mugful's a distant memory? What was she doing? As they slowly pulled away, she crossed her arms. His voice, husky with emotion, bid her goodnight.

Although Taylor didn't need anything complicated like a relationship, Brent had her mind reeling in directions she wasn't used to traveling. Her life was complete, wasn't it? She didn't need a man. So why was she all jittery inside? Why did she yearn to be in his arms again?

Getting involved with him wasn't smart. Not at all.

THE NEXT WEEK passed quickly. On the evenings Taylor didn't go out with Brent, she searched for the ring. All she found for her efforts so far were trinkets from her childhood and a gold tie clip that had belonged to her grandfather.

Brent continued to bring her breakfast each morning, and at her urging, he even grew accustomed to her favorite coffee. Taylor had returned the extra door key so he could let himself in when she wasn't around.

Deep down, she enjoyed the playful interactions with him, the flirtation and kisses, and even more so, the way his warm arms wrapped around her and hugged her as no one could. She convinced herself that when all the work was done, she would go home to Raleigh. Life would return to normal. Mr. Roberts would be a fond memory, a recollection she could pull from when things became stressed. After all, Taylor Harrison *needed* no one.

THE DAY HAD been a washout as far as Brent was concerned. The new materials he'd ordered were late. So late that he sent the crew to another job, deciding to drive into town and research what caused the delay. "Taylor, I have to track down some supplies. Would you like to go with me?"

"Um…" Fiddling with her ponytail, she muttered, "I need to finish up a report this morning and gather more of Granny's Kay's things. Then I have to tackle cleaning out the attic. No, I'd better stay here today."

Later, after Brent left, Taylor ventured into the hallway upstairs. The entryway to the attic was at the very end of the passage. Taylor opened the creaky old door and sneezed at the dust that flew by. As she ascended the steps, she waved her hands, tearing down cobwebs that had formed across the walkway. Once inside the room, she flipped on the light and circled around, overwhelmed at the number of boxes scattered about. Who knew what they contained? The packages were going to have to be sorted—that would be a job in itself. The old pieces of furniture she planned to have hauled off.

Taylor lined up assorted light fixture covers and toys she had found. Perched in the back of the open room was an odd end table, a bookshelf, and her old baby bed. She added a couple of wooden chairs to the mix. Finally, with the wall of oddities built, she was ready to begin the chore of toting them to the hall—a workout far more intense than any the gym could provide. Brent had offered help, so her plans were to ask him if he would carry those items to the landfill.

Next, she tackled the boxes. Most of them were packed with old records, tapes, and outdated electronics. Taylor wasn't going to deal with the hassle of seeing if any of the stuff was worth selling. That would take time, and she didn't care to spend countless hours contemplating unused bits and pieces that her grandparents discarded years ago. As the day wore on, she toted boxes to the kitchen, thankful the cartons hadn't amounted to as many as she'd believed. She would sort out the contents that evening, looking for the ring, and then haul anything reusable to the nearest thrift store the next day.

BRENT WALKED INTO the area and eyed the dusty boxes scattered throughout the kitchen. "Do you need help with any of these?"

Taylor sat Indian style on the floor, sorting a box. "These are from the attic. The pile over by the table is trash, and this stack will be sent to a secondhand store. Could you take the old pieces of furniture I put in the upstairs hall down to the veranda, so I can get them hauled off?"

Brent extended his hand to help Taylor climb from her sitting position. "If you like, I can get the guys to load the mess into my truck. I'll haul it away when I leave. You have a long job ahead."

Before he turned to leave, he planted a light kiss on her lips. "I'll be back around seven with some take-out from Captain Fillet. We can hang out. You can finally tell me why a pretty, smart woman like Taylor Harrison hasn't married some lucky man."

She hesitated for a second. "Okay, thanks for lending a hand. That would be great, Brent."

AT SIX-THIRTY TAYLOR immerged from the shower. She slipped into jeans and a V-neck tee, glad that Brent was returning with fish. After the men left, she had worked all afternoon grouping the things in the boxes. She had three piles—a disposal stack, a giveaway load, and a couple of small containers that would go back to her condominium. She found a lot of her baby clothes, school papers, and homemade cards she'd drawn for her grandparents and parents. Everything except a sapphire ring.

CHAPTER FIVE

THE NEXT DAY Brent showed up at his regular time. Around lunch, he strolled into one of the rooms downstairs to find Taylor taping up a cardboard box. "Yesterday I went to the hardware store to check on the flooring, and the clerk told me he couldn't get all the order in by the date I need it. They have a shade darker in stock, so I could pick it up today. I need you to ride with me and see if the color is okay."

Taylor straightened from her stooped position on the floor and stretched her back. "I remember the other shade. The darker hue will work fine. Let me stay and finish this room while you pick up the order."

Brent scanned the room full of empty totes she had waiting to be filled with Kay's knick-knacks and nodded in support of her decision. As he walked to the truck, his mind was on Taylor. *She's not only pretty and smart, she's a hard worker, even for her family.*

TAYLOR AMBLED FROM one room to another. The difference mesmerized her. A fresh coat of paint and new light fixtures went a long way in brightening up the rooms. Taylor admired the transformation taking place. Now that the walls had been partially removed, she could visualize what the open area would look like.

A high-pitched ding-a-ling sound ricocheted in the empty room. Taylor glanced around, searching for the sound and followed the racket to the foyer. Brent's cell phone lay buzzing a tune on the hall table.

"Hello?" She listened to muffled sounds of crying that resonated from the other end of the cell phone. Not knowing what to say, Taylor settled for another, louder, "Hello?"

A woman's brittle voice quivered. "Is this Taylor? It's Daisy." After a moment and another trembling breath, she whimpered. "A car hit this poor little dog and left it lying in front of my store. I need to see if Brent can take it over to my husband's office for a checkup. I can't leave the shop right now. I'm waiting for a gentleman to come by. He wants to see the store, maybe purchase it. I tried to call his cell to postpone, but I'm getting no answer. George's receptionist said they are swamped and she can't break away. Taylor, I'm afraid for the dog—he's in a bad condition. I hoped Brent would help." Daisy's speech broke up into syllables as she attempted to calm herself. "I...can't...stand...seeing...anything suffer. Do you know where he is?"

Taylor took a deep breath. "He went to get some supplies. He forgot his phone. I don't know when he'll be back. I could call the store and track him down, but he also mentioned other stops along the way. He's been gone a while. I'm afraid there's just no way to contact him."

"Oh, dear. I have to take this dog to the vet. Can you—?"

I hate dogs. After that bite from a stray, and all the shots that followed, she didn't trust them. *But I have to help...* Taylor hoped she wouldn't regret her next words. "Daisy, I'll be right over."

Taylor rubbed her face with her free hand. Squeezing her eyes shut, she shook her head. "I can do this. It's just a dog."

TAYLOR VEERED INTO a parking space, slammed the car door behind her, and found Daisy outside kneeling over a blond-colored mutt. Blood ran down the side of the dog's mouth. Taylor rushed across the lot but stopped several feet away, keeping her distance. "The dog looks bad. What are you going to do?"

The older lady glanced at Taylor, then at the small lump laying at the curbside. "Will you take the dog to George's office? It's not far. The lady who works part-time isn't here today. I need to keep my appointment if I'm ever going to get this dress shop sold."

Taylor's heart beat faster as she eyed the dog lying on its side. It looked barely alive, but Taylor didn't want to touch it. She certainly didn't want the animal in her car. What might a hurt creature do inside a moving vehicle? Attack her while she was driving? "Daisy, I....you know the way, and you know animals better than I do. You take the dog, and I'll show the man around. I'm good with people and business matters. If he has any questions I can't answer, I'll write them down so you can call him later this evening."

Daisy looked at the lump of fur, then at Taylor. "I know you said you once worked at a store. I'm confident you can show him around and handle matters sufficiently. I promise it will only be for a while. I'll drop off the dog and stay long enough to find out what's wrong."

TAYLOR PACED THE floor, straightening racks and watching the clock. The potential buyer arrived right on the hour. Taylor explained that the owner had an emergency and had to leave, then gave him a tour. Together, they checked the facilities and the stock room.

On the counter, Daisy left a few papers for the man to examine concerning the taxes and zoning. Taylor took notes of his questions and told him Daisy would call him that evening.

After a while, Taylor decided if she had to be there, she may as well sort clothes from the box Daisy had been working through.

While she was busy hanging the new summer skirts, customers ventured in. Thirty-five minutes later, Taylor had mastered the cash register, thankful that Daisy had one of the older models.

For the next hour, she stood at the back wall, helping a woman search through the dresses for the perfect one to wear to a party. Just as she was checking her out, Daisy walked into the store.

"Thank you so much, Taylor. I don't know what I would have done if you hadn't stepped in. My husband stopped the bleeding and fixed the dog's broken leg. I believe the little pooch will be fine." She laughed, adding, "It seems that if no one claims the dog, I'll have a new addition to our family."

WHAT AN AFTERNOON. Taylor stepped across the threshold of her grandmother's house. With hammers thumping upstairs, she made a quick trip to her bedroom and retrieved her laptop. Even though it was late in the day, she was armed with a desire to work.

Sitting down at the table, she logged into her reports but found herself bored, distracted by the little dress shop and the customers who'd stopped by. The atmosphere was completely different from her routine at Mugful's. *Spending time at the boutique was nice. I still enjoy the customer service end of retail.*

Brent's voice rang out, startling her. "Daisy just called and told me what you did for her. Thanks for helping. She's always been a softy for animals. I know you're busy, but having you watch the dress shop meant a lot to my sister."

"It was my pleasure."

"Still, I appreciate it. Let me know how I can repay you, please."

"No need."

"I know that cost you needed time."

"In Galatians, there's a verse that says 'Carry each other's burdens, and in this way you will fulfill the law of Christ.' I was just acting as any Christian should."

Taylor put her hand to her lips. Where had that come from? It had been a long time since she focused on God's words.

"You're a sweet lady. You try to hide it, but you're not fooling me."

She slid him a smile. "Maybe the sweet side is the act."

"Not a chance."

TAYLOR SPENT THE next few days traveling to Raleigh to tie up some loose ends with a store opening in another state. On Thursday evening, before the new floor was to be laid, Brent and his crew finished up their day early and left.

Taylor wandered around the downstairs area. Her job of searching the ground floor was almost over, and no ring had been found. Walking through the main living area had her admiring the way the room looked. There were no walls now, and the sun from the big window shone bright, shimmering across the floor.

Following the path of the light, she noticed a gap in the floor boards under the window. Taylor walked over and peered into the narrow slit between the boards. She couldn't spot anything that looked as if it had been dropped into the gash. Still… Her imagination had her wanting to investigate anyway. The boards were too close together for her to stick her finger in, so she decided to get a flat object to poke inside. Taylor went to the kitchen and returned with a knife. Crouching down on her knees, she dug in the small gap and tried to feel for any object that shouldn't be there.

While she was prodding with the sharp blade, Brent strolled back into the room. "What are you doing?"

The sudden sound ricocheted in the empty area. Taylor's hand jerked, causing the knife to slip.

Grasping the injury the blade inflicted, she yelled "Ouch!" while blood gushed from the cut. Brent rushed to her side, snatching a handkerchief from his pocket. "Taylor, let me." In careful strokes, he patted the gash, inspecting the wound. A gentleness she had never heard before sounded in his voice. "What in the world were you trying to do?"

Before she could answer, he pulled her to her feet and guided her toward the kitchen sink. Without any words, he wet a paper towel and tenderly cleaned the wound. "Do you have any bandages or ointment?"

Taylor raised her head, embarrassed by the situation. "In my room. There are first-aid supplies in the bathroom cabinet." Brent disappeared into the bedroom and returned with antiseptic and a Band-Aid. Then he seated her at the table, applied the cream, and dressed her hand. Afterward, he planted a tender kiss on the doctored mishap.

Quietly, he sat a glass of tea in front of her and straddled the chair beside her. "Now, tell me what you were doing poking the floor with a knife?"

She took a deep breath and stalled for a few seconds. *He'll think searching for the ring is trivial and useless. I did.*

To Granny Kay, though, it's not.

But she needed to offer him an explanation. Taylor looked into his eyes. "I was searching for something."

Shaking his head, his words came out in a measured tone. "You were looking for something in the floor with a very sharp object?"

Taylor rubbed her temple with her good hand. "My grandmother sent me here not just to pack, but to search the place. To hunt for a lost ring."

Brent rose from the chair and pointed to the cut. "So all this over a little ring?"

She stood and met his gaze. "It's a special ring, at least to my grandmother. It's an heirloom that belonged to her mother and generations of my family before her."

"Where did she lose it? I'll help."

Always so sweet, so helpful. Inhaling a deep breath, she shrugged. "It's not that simple."

"What do you mean it's not simple? Your grandmother lost a ring. We'll find it for her." As if the subject was closed, he added, "I came back here this evening to ask you go to Tally's restaurant with me. It's a good place to eat. Can we talk about this over some country cooking?"

AS THEY SHARED the meal, Brent talked of his life, and the conversation steered to a time a few years earlier, when he asked Jesus to forgive his sins.

"So you just decided you wanted to get saved?" With curiosity, Taylor looked across the table at him.

"No, it wasn't that easy. God had to catch me first. For years, I went to church with my aunt. During that time, I never did more than show up. I'd sit and wonder why all my friends seemed to have a home and family, and I was still trotting around by myself. I had my company but wanted more. God kept nudging my heart. I began to realize that a relationship with Jesus was one of the things I was missing. That's when I got saved. Since then, I've realized God has my life in control. Things will work out for his glory. The way you live changes when you're saved. I cleaned up my act. Now I'm trying to be the way I believe Jesus wants me. People will always struggle with worldly situations. Problems and temptations always try to get you down. It's easier to cope with those situations if the Lord's by your side."

Taylor wiggled in her seat. Something about his words tugged at her, pulled her emotions. "I always went to church with my grandmother when I was young. I got saved before I graduated from college. Now, though, my life has become hectic. It seems like I don't have time for such things. I guess you could say I'm a backslider. For the past five years, Granny Kay has made excuses to get me to accompany her to church at least once a month. She even bribes me with donuts. That was before she broke her hip. I guess my excuse is that Sunday is the only day I have to relax. I use the day to lounge around my condo and read."

The uneasy tone in Taylor's voice raised questions in Brent's mind. He started to tell her that God is always there, waiting for the backslider to return to the fold. He didn't know why, but all of a sudden he found himself changing the subject. He didn't want to push her. "What do you like to read?"

Taylor put her fork down and contemplated the answer. For reasons unknown, she didn't want to divulge all her reading preferences. "I enjoy a good suspense, but…"

"But? Be honest, now."

"Well, my passion is love stories."

"Love stories? Now this is intriguing."

"It's silly."

"It's not. Tell me more. Lords and ladies? Cowboys and spinster schoolmarms?"

"You sound like *you* read a lot of paperbacks."

"My sister. And she loves to share. Well?"

"I like small-town romance." More to herself than Brent, she mumbled, "I enjoy reading about quaint communities and couples finding love. Families coming together. Corny, I know. Happily-ever-after endings are nice."

"They are. We all want one, don't we?" For a moment, their gazes locked. "About your grandmother's ring. Where did she lose it?"

"Well…" Wiping her mouth with a napkin, she sat down her fork. The tale of the murder rolled off of her tongue.

"Wow, that's some story. I doubt the ring will ever be found. A lot of years have gone by."

"Yes, I know. I figured that as long as I have to pack and clean out the house, I may as well search for it. At least I can tell Granny Kay I tried."

Agreeing with her, Brent added, "I'll keep my eyes open. It would be nice to find it for Kay."

STANDING ON THE large porch, Brent unlocked the door for Taylor. When she turned around to say goodbye, he stepped closer. "I enjoy being with you. When we first met, I thought we were so different. We're really not. Both of us have distinct lives..." He stood near and gently rubbed her neck. "But I think we have some common ground too. For example, we're both determined people. Hardworking, and we care about helping our families."

All day he had thought about this woman. The night before, Brent had prayed about the situation. Somehow, without him realizing it, Taylor had wormed herself in his heart, and now he didn't want to lose her. He was aware of her commitment to her job. Nevertheless, he was compelled to believe she was the lady he wanted.

"I know we haven't talked much about the way we see our futures. Somehow, I get the feeling that, deep down, each of us needs the same things. It's going to be a journey, you and me. We don't know what God's plans are yet." Brent looked intently in her eyes. "Taylor, what *do* you want? At the end of the day, when your head hits the pillow, what do you fantasize about? Only work? Don't you think you'll ever want a family?"

Taylor swallowed hard, her emotions torn between desire and fear. Her heart wanted to believe she and Brent could have something more. Her head told her that despite those few traits in common that he'd named, they were two different people. He was just like the other men she had known and would expect her to give up everything she'd worked for. "Sometimes I think the things I want are what fairytales are made of. Maybe one day I would like a family. I enjoy my career, though." She looked away. "I don't understand how some women seem to have it all and be happy."

Brent looped his arms around her and held her close. She leaned into him as he moved his hands down her back. Her heart hammered against her chest as he kissed the side of her neck and whispered. "With God on your side, you *can* have it all."

When he released her, he flashed that crooked smile and pushed a loose strand of hair behind her ear. Then, without saying a word, he turned and walked into the night.

Taylor touched her lips as she watched him leave. All he ever did was kiss her and hold her close. The guy remained a gentleman. What's more, his arms made her feel…cherished. Protected. How easy it would be to stay in them, if he never let her go.

She turned to go into the house, wondering why simple hugs and kisses had her reacting this way. These dates with Brent were a huge lapse in judgment. His presence in her life had begun to make her question things she didn't want to address. *Talk about a whopper of a mistake. What am I doing?*

TAYLOR JUST FINISHED her e-mails when the phone rang.

"Hi, sweetheart. How's everything going?"

Taylor filled her grandmother in on the renovations until the older woman interrupted to ask about the ring search. "Granny Kay, I've hunted through the downstairs over and over, and I haven't found any ring. I still have a couple of rooms upstairs to comb through. I think it's a lost cause. I'm sorry."

"What about Brent?"

For some reason, the tone of her grandmother's voice piqued her suspicions. Taylor refused to acknowledge such a silly course of thought and paid no attention, shoving all her misgivings aside. "I suppose you were right when you told me once not to judge a book by its cover. He's not as bad as I thought."

"That's good, dear, because I need you to stay longer. I've been talking to a realtor, and he thinks we need to increase the size of the closet in the master bedroom. I've asked Brent about adding space, and he thinks he has a solution. The job should take only a couple days."

Protests ran amuck in her mind. Only her respect for her grandmother stifled the outburst. Barely controlling her words, she said goodbye and hung up.

The cell phone slammed hard on the table. Taylor's brows creased as curse words escaped her lips and ran together in exasperation. Sarcastically, she repeated, "Take only a couple days."

To her grandmother, time was nothing. Even though Taylor had personal days to take, her boss acted as if he had something on his mind of late. She needed to get back to her office fulltime. Other than her love for her grandmother, Mugful's was top priority.

A shout of exasperation wailed from her throat. Then words so often spoken in her presence flitted into her mind...something about carrying each other's burdens.

That was all she needed now—more advice from the Bible. Quotes she'd heard her grandmother repeat one too many times.

TO TAYLOR'S SURPRISE, the days flew by. She busied herself with hauling away the rest of the boxes and paraphernalia she considered trash. The few places she hoped she would find the jewelry proved a dead-end.

Regardless of her best efforts to avoid him, she continued to date Brent. A new longing started to bud. Ideas formed in her mind, teasing her with possibilities of a relationship, of a marriage. Like a whirlwind, her reactions to him teetered back and forth, going from impossible to outrageous. Taylor tried hard to stomp out any fantasies about her and Brent, no matter what her desire tried to tell her.

A lot of feelings may have been stirred. Things happened in a short time. Ultimately, nothing was any different. Her life was the same—or would be in a few days, when she returned to her condo in Raleigh.

CHAPTER SIX

"THE CREW AND I are done for the day. I framed in a portion in the main bedroom for additional storage. As I was refiguring the layout, I noticed part of the wood flooring in that room is rotted out. Before I can finish the closet, the floor will need to be patched. I plan on repairing that tomorrow."

Brent studied Taylor, searching her face for a sign, a clue as to how she felt about him. He yearned for her smile, that special way her eyes seemed only for him. The past few nights when they went out, he had hinted toward a permanent relationship. He very much wanted to continue seeing Taylor, even if she did live an hour's drive away. A little traveling distance was nothing. "I'm sending the crew to another job site. I can finish up here. Renovations will be completed by the end of the week."

Brent walked around the table, closing the distance between them. He feared she'd push him away, shut him out. She'd made it plain that the thought of a relationship made her skittish. "After all this is done, can I call you? Can we continue to see each other?"

She walked away and stood on the other side of the cabinets to place distance between them. She too wasted hours the night before, considering that very question. Wondering if she had time for the distractions a man like Brent caused. Should she chance a serious relationship? A broken heart?

"I do like you, Brent. It's just...my world is so hectic right now." As if dismissing him, she added, "I stay busy with my job. I don't see it working."

"Taylor, I don't see what the problem is."

"That's exactly the problem. You don't understand. My career means a lot to me. You assume if you charm me well enough, I'll cast it aside. I won't. My career is all I've got outside of Granny Kay. Let's not do this, Brent. You can't fix everything. Some things are meant to be, and others aren't."

TAYLOR CALLED HER grandmother and filled her in on the progress with the upgrades. Granny Kay mentioned she wanted to come and see the improvements, but Taylor worried about her healing.

"Granny Kay, you don't have to come out here. I can take pictures for you. I'm sorry about the ring. I plan to look upstairs in the last room left later tonight. I think maybe years ago the killer lied. The ring's nowhere to be found. That or someone else stole it. Maybe Elizabeth lost it down the drain or something and was afraid to say."

"You sound unsettled. Is everything all right? How have you and Brent been getting along?"

Taylor hesitated, wondering why it made any difference how she and the man who was hired to remodel the house got along. "We went out a few times, and he's a nice guy. Why do you ask?"

"Well, I was hoping you would like Louise's nephew, and the two of you could become friends. He's a nice Christian man, and there's more to life than that job, you know."

"Her *nephew?* Why didn't you tell me?" Taylor groaned. "I know what you're up to! Matchmaking on top of it all. You need to understand Brent's life is here, and mine is in the city. Besides, you know the long hours I work. I don't have time for a steady relationship."

The older woman's speech cracked, sounding timid. "I wanted you to make up your own mind about him, without any influences on my part. You keep saying you don't have time for a relationship. Hun, I know a lot of people who have busy lives and commute from Liberty Cove to Raleigh daily."

LATER IN THE day, Brent ambled into the kitchen. Taylor looked up from her laptop, and her eyes narrowed. "Brent Roberts, how dare you keep the truth from me? Did you think you could trick me? You should have told me from the get-go. You men are all alike."

Brent stopped in his tracks. He wasn't shocked by Taylor speaking her mind—he knew she was a strong-willed woman. Yet he couldn't understand *why* she was yelling at him. He eyeballed her in wonder. What had he lied about? "I haven't misled you about anything. Neither would I lie to you, nor anyone, for that matter."

"You should have told me from the beginning that Louise is your aunt. Instead, you let me worry about some strange man being in the house and doing my grandmother's repairs. I never needed to stay here!"

Brent held back the smile that threatened. In spite of Taylor being upset, he found her reaction humorous. He especially liked the way one of her eyebrows hiked up when she voiced her distress.

"I thought you were aware from the start. I figured Kay told you before you arrived. That's why I considered your reaction to me kind of funny when we first met." He stepped closer and lowered his voice. "I wouldn't keep anything from you, not on purpose, anyway. I'm sorry about the misunderstanding."

He picked up one of her curls. "I hope you won't stay mad. It was only an oversight."

Taylor swiped his hand away. She tapped her foot and glared at him.

Stepping back a little, Brent grinned. "Taylor, please. It was only a misunderstanding."

"You're infuriating! 'Only a misunderstanding.'" Taylor mocked his words. "No one but me is going to map out my life." She stormed into the bedroom and slammed the door.

THAT EVENING AFTER dinner alone, Taylor wandered around the house. Since the last room was going to be completed soon, she intended to finish her hunt tonight. That would leave tomorrow for her to clean out the guest quarters where she was staying.

The conversation with her grandmother clung to her thoughts. She shelved the information about Brent being Louise's nephew. In the end, no harm was done, even if the misunderstanding—as Brent called it—made her mad. She would have preferred to have received the information from the beginning.

She couldn't decide if dating Brent on a permanent basis was something she even wanted, and she didn't care to think about the other things her grandmother said about her future. She'd worked hard to get where she was. Her job was important to her, and she had a good life now—without complications. Brent would most assuredly a difficulty. *Except I really like the guy.*

TWO HOURS LATER, she marched into the master bedroom, the last place she needed to search. It was a nice size, but she agreed it needed more closet space. The men had boxed off a section of the wall and framed around the spot for additional shelving. Taylor surveyed the results, approving, and then peeked into the opening at the far end. She eyed the cavity and stooped down, looking at a hole caused by the decayed wood. A jagged crack ran along the floor. She was about to push herself up when something glittered. A strange sparkle of light illuminated from the slit in the planks. Taylor squinted, focusing her vision inside the dark cavity.

The gash between the planks wasn't large enough for her fingers, so retrieving whatever caused that glint would be a hassle. The idea entered her mind to wait until tomorrow. When Brent cut away the decayed wood, she'd easily be able to pull out whatever it was. But it might fall through and roll away. One more glimpse at the spot incited too much curiosity. That glistening object could be a ring. Then again, she had found several shiny objects—pieces of her and her grandparents' lives scattered throughout the house—and none of those remains had been the one thing she needed to find.

Taylor stood, feeling defeated. Doubtful it was anything more than some silver childhood bauble. This was the last room—except for the one she slept in—and no heirloom ring. Of course, she never expected to find her grandmother's lost ring, though deep inside she couldn't stop herself from harboring hope.

She retreated toward the door. "May as well check it out. It's probably nothing. We'll see. Then tomorrow I'll look around in the room I'm staying in."

Heading down the steps, she went in search of a flashlight and some kind of tool to dig in the small space. Taylor hurried to the kitchen and jerked open the cabinet drawer, searching the barren spot that only held a steak knife, spoon, and fork. She picked up a sharp utensil, but the red area on her hand where her wound had been forced her to reconsider. Not a good idea.

She threw down the knife and slammed the drawer closed. What to use? Turning, she scanned the room, looking for anything to help grab hold of her find. "Aha!" Taylor smiled as she remembered a toolbox sitting upstairs.

Back in the empty room, she rummaged through Brent's tools and found a flashlight. She picked through different items. There had to be something in the big metal container to use to grab hold of whatever lay there.

She was about to give up when she spotted a pair of needle-nose pliers. Grabbing the light and tool, she headed to the hole in the floor.

Taking her time, Taylor worked diligently, opening and closing the long narrow device and grasping at whatever twinkled in the light. She held her breath in anticipation, clamping down on part of what appeared to be a wide band that gleamed against the dark wood. Just as she was about to bring the shimmering circle out of the tiny space, it slipped, landing sideways in the small opening. No, it wouldn't come out that way. The opening wasn't big enough.

Taylor made several more failed attempts and stretched her legs out on the floor in exhaustion. Leaning back on the palms of her hands, she stared at the ceiling for several minutes in weariness as she considered the possibilities. If this was indeed the ring, she could just picture her grandmother's joyous reaction.

That inkling fueled her with more determination. Once again she started the chore of retrieving what had to be a ring—of some sort anyway.

Taylor grabbed the band with the tool and held on. She twisted her hand so it was upright while she held tight. Her knuckles hurt from the grip she maintained on the pliers. With a slow, steady pull, the ring emerged from its grave. Taylor ogled the stone. *I found it!*

Her squeal of delight pierced the room. Taylor closed her hand around the band, leaping to her feet. She jumped for joy, her shouts of elation ringing out into the empty room. "Thank you, Jesus, thank you! I found Granny Kay's ring." She squeezed her eyes shut against the overwhelming excitement and enfolded the treasure in her clutches. On impulse, she held the ring close to her heart and said another deeper prayer of thanks to God for allowing her to find her grandmother's cherished possession.

Taylor continued to grip the band close to her body and turned with a quick motion toward the door. Dizziness overtook her. Woozy, she grabbed the frame at the entrance to steady her swaying body. Surely just a reaction from all the excitement. Taylor stood motionless for a moment to get her balance and then trotted downstairs to call her grandmother.

She ran into her room and picked up her cell phone. As she slid it open, she realized it was midnight—much too late to call. While Grandmother might not mind, given the news, Taylor didn't want to wake her host. The good news was just going to have to wait until tomorrow morning.

Sitting on the side of her bed, Taylor gawked at the ring. She had to admit the piece of jewelry was stunning. The white gold shank boasted the darkest square sapphire she had ever seen.

As she twisted the jewelry around, light caught the stone. The nugget illuminated, sparkling, as if taking on a life force of its own. She stared at her discovery, wondering how anything so dark-colored could glow with so much brightness.

Taylor easily slipped the ring on her finger. A bolt of energy shot up her arm. Electricity danced to her shoulder, causing it to tingle. Her hand jerked. The sensation of being jabbed by a thousand needles pricked her body. She wheezed in a shaky breath, heart racing as she stepped back and caressed her hand. What had just happened?

Taylor walked on quivering legs to her bed, staggering a bit. Falling onto her mattress, she rubbed her eyes. The pounding in her chest continued. Taylor forced herself to take slow breaths. The reaction must be from all the excitement. The sheer elation of the moment caused her blood pressure to rise.

She decided to remove the ring from her finger and place it somewhere safe. But the band wouldn't budge. Taylor twisted the ring with all the force she could muster. It didn't move.

For ten minutes at the sink, with the drain plugged, Taylor asserted every effort she could think of. She used lotion, then soap, tugging at the wide circle, pulling it toward her fingertips.

How could the ring be so small after it slid on her finger so easily?

Ten minutes later, the skin of her finger was raw and inflamed. Redness showed around the band from all the abuse she'd put her hand through. It would just have to stay put—for tonight anyway. At least the once-lost possession wasn't going anywhere.

Taylor lay down, her heartbeat steady now, with just an occasional flutter. Turning over in bed, she smiled. Her stomach churned with enthusiasm at the wonderful news she was going to share with her grandmother.

CHAPTER SEVEN

TAYLOR PLUMMETED FROM her precarious position on the edge of the countertop. Falling, falling...landing in his arms. His gaze penetrated hers as he held her close, testing her reaction. She felt her skin tingle in eagerness while he moved forward, seeking her lips. How she wanted to stay there, enclosed in her husband's arms forever...

Taylor bolted upright, awakened from her dream. In an angry gesture, she balled her fist and punched the pillow. Running her hands through her mass of curls, she glared into the darkness that embodied the room, stunned at what her subconscious had conjured up.

Her husband?

Now more than ever, she was certain Brent wasn't the man she needed in her life. The only complication she wanted was her career. She'd tried, but relationships never worked out for her. Brent was such a distraction that she was now losing sleep.

She flopped down on her pillow and turned over, kicking at the blanket in an attempt to forget the dream and any desires the scene planted in her mind.

An hour later, Taylor was still tossing in bed. Rest refused to come. The memory of her last failed relationship hovered in her mind. Since the breakup, she'd made a promise to herself. When she did get involved with another man, he would share her outlook on life about business and success. He'd be a man who realized, and appreciated, that women had ambitions.

She continued turning over in bed, trying to find a comfortable position. For the first time in months, she couldn't help thinking about Lee. A year ago, she had been certain he was the right man for her. How wrong she'd been.

The last time they were together was at Mugful's annual Christmas party. There, she overheard the cutting remarks Lee used as he talked to her assistant, downgrading the value of women and their worth in business. He didn't realize until later that she was in the doorway, listening.

That night she discovered the hard way that Lee believed men were the only ones who had anything to contribute in society. The conversation still numbed her. Lee made it clear that he saw women as a decoration made to boost a man's image, and a long-term relationship with him was intended to end with her vacuuming in pearls, wiping his children's faces, and organizing his brown-nosing parties. The stupid narrow-mindedness of some men. No way! The next time she was involved with anyone, they would respect her for her abilities.

Taylor's mind shifted to Brent and his crooked smile. Sure, he seemed to have made a success out of the construction business. Although…he just didn't appear to take things in life seriously. Even though they had spent time together, she wondered exactly what warped beliefs he possessed about females—beliefs she didn't know about.

TAYLOR SAT AT the table, staring into her espresso, her laptop forgotten. Over and over, she replayed the conversation with her grandmother and her reaction. For the first time in years, she had heard her grandmother yell out in glee. The happiness in her voice made the time off work worthwhile. Never in her career had she felt so accomplished.

Brent marched in, carrying the usual white paper bag from the nearest fast-food joint. "Good morning. You look tired."

Brent immediately noticed a flicker of light from a ring he hadn't seen her wear before. He pointed to her hand. "Is that the ring you were looking for?"

She smoothed her hair, showing the efforts of an attempted smile. "I found it last night in the rotten floorboards upstairs. Only trouble is, I slid it on my finger. Now I can't seem to get it off. I suppose I'll have to wear it until I can get to jewelers. Can you believe I located it?"

He leaned against the counter and observed the puffiness under her eyes. "You stayed up all night looking for it?"

"No, I had a bad dream. Well, it wasn't *bad*, just…bothersome. I tossed and turned awhile before I got back to sleep." Despite the beverage she'd been nursing, Taylor's throat went dry. An irresistible urge to blurt out secret hopes itched in her throat. The need to tell him she never wanted to leave mounted from somewhere deep within, begging to be released. She placed her hand on her neck and swallowed hard. Taylor fought the temptation to say things she wasn't sure needed to be said. Ever. By sheer will, she forced herself to stay in the seat and control the compulsion to wrap her arms around him and hold on.

Brent picked up a breakfast sandwich. "I'll fix the floor today and get started on closing in the closet. It should be finished by tomorrow. Then I guess you'll be on your way back to Raleigh."

He took a bite and chewed. After he swallowed, Brent cleared his throat. "I've enjoyed the time we spent together. I hope it doesn't end just because you live a few miles away."

Brent waited for her to say something, but all she did was look at him like a deer blinded by car lights.

"Are you okay? Taylor, sometimes we have to step away from our safety zone and give things a chance."

"These few weeks have been good. Maybe we both needed this little diversion. But life goes on."

He stood and his footsteps smacked the hardwood floor as he stalked away. She listened to the thump of heavy steps as he headed up the stairs.

Taylor rose and paced the floor, twisting the ring on her finger. Why had such a reaction come over her? What in the world was wrong with her?

KAY SAT AT the kitchen table, watching Louise as she loaded the dishwasher, wishing her bad hip didn't prevent her from being helpful. "Louise, guess what? I spoke with Taylor this morning. She found the ring."

A wide smile crossed Louise's face as she turned, giving her friend her full attention. "That's wonderful! Why aren't you more excited?"

"It is wonderful." Kay grinned then dropped her gaze and concentrated on the floral design printed on the plate she'd just eaten eggs and bacon from. "Oh, Louise, I'm glad she found the ring. I was so happy when she told me. To think, after all these years, I get to see the family jewel again. It's just...well...now it's over. I wanted her to find something else more important in life too."

Louise tossed down the sponge she'd used to wipe the top of the stove. "Kay Harrison, I'm surprised! When have you ever given up on God? You of all people should know the Lord works things out in his own incredible, mysterious way. You can't force change! Remember the verse in Matthew? It tells us that *if* we have faith, then He answers our prayers." Louise moved to sit next to her friend. "Kay, you told me once that you came from a long line of faith-filled women who prayed their way through problems. That stanza in Mark talks about removing mountains. Jesus tells us to believe that things will come to pass. Right now, our mountain is Taylor's obsession with that demanding job. Also, I think we both have come to suspect she and Brent are meant for each other. She just needs to slow down and realize it for herself." With a sound of finality in her voice, Louise stood again and set to work wiping the table. "With the help of our Lord, she will. There is nothing magical about it. We just trust in God and believe in a positive outcome."

A renewed smile lit Kay's face. "Yes, you're right. I do need to keep in mind that the Lord works things out. He always has. I have to take into account the parable in the Bible about the lady who went to the king, pleading with him to help her get out of her distress. The ruler finally assisted her, and it was because she troubled him for days. I plan to stand on God's word and pray until He gets tired of listening to old Kay Harrison."

TAYLOR SPENT MOST of the day straightening the guest room, preparing to depart the next afternoon. She left a towel and tomorrow's change of clothes on top of her suitcase. Brent tried to convince her to go out with him, but she declined, using the excuse of a headache. Brent was a complication in her life, and she didn't know to deal with the emotions his presence created. Taylor couldn't recall the last time a man had turned her inside out, especially when they had only kissed.

Taylor sighed, turning down the covers. Tomorrow night she would be in Raleigh, at home and in her own bed. Then things would sort themselves out. The time she had spent with Brent Roberts would slowly fade away, as all summer romances do.

HER BREATHING LABORED. Taylor jogged down the hallway. The more she moved forward, the longer the hallway stretched. Nothing was wrong—she sensed that was so—but her actions confused her. Why couldn't she reach the door?

She glanced over her shoulder, finding the entrance to her office behind her. There loomed her boss, waving for her to return. The distance to the elevator kept growing farther away. Harder and harder she pushed, slowly gaining ground. Why was she so determined to escape the job she loved? But she had to. When she finally reached the entryway, warmth washed over her and she took a step inside. Her foot slipped and caused her tumble, right into Brent's waiting arms.

Taylor jerked her eyes open. What was that? Reaching up, she rubbed her forehead and swiped the sweaty hair out of her face. The bed covers lay in a heap around her ankles. Frustrated, she pushed them to the floor and sat on the side of the bed. *Crazy.* With a huff of air, she stomped toward the shower. Over and over, her mind played out the dream. Taylor only hoped her dawn would prove better than the night had been. Either that or it was going to be a terrible day.

SIPPING HER COFFEE, Taylor glanced at the ring on her finger. The band caught the morning light. Watching the gemstone, she could almost swear the color had flashed bright in the streak of sun that shone through the window. The sound of a truck tore her attention away. She strolled to the foyer, watching Brent pull in the driveway.

His long legs devouring the distance between them, he walked up the steps with his usual offer of breakfast and smiled as he leaned toward her, planting a kiss quick on her lips. Brent handed her the bag containing with two muffins.

"Thanks. Fresh coffee is in the kitchen." Taylor took the container. On the outside, she ignored the kiss. As if he had done nothing, she followed him toward the smell of the caffeinated beverage.

Brent filled two cups and placed one in front of her. "I should be done today. Before I leave, you'll need to look over the work. If you believe everything is to your grandmother's specifications, sign the work release, and the house will be completed. I'll be finished."

"I hope not with me." Out of the blue, the unexpected words filled the kitchen.

He jerked his head toward her. "What did you say?"

What was wrong with her? Where in the world did that comment come from? Taylor's face grew hot. All she could think to do was downplay the situation. "Hum…nothing. Don't pay me any attention. I haven't slept much in the past two days. I'm sure all the work will be fine."

Brent looked at her long and hard. Before he headed toward his duties, he dug a card out of his front pocket and tossed it on the table. "I heard what you said. I don't want us to be finished either. You know I'm just a phone call away, and I drive to Raleigh often. I would like for us to see each other regularly. Making the trip is nothing for me."

Once alone, she picked up Brent's trade card and slipped it into her pocket. Pacing the kitchen floor, she toyed with the band on her finger, twisting it. A fear of what other words might fly out of her mouth before she left hovered above her like a rain cloud. What made her voice such a silly thing anyway? Had she been thinking out loud?

TAYLOR FOLLOWED BRENT through the house, touring the empty rooms and examining the renovations. No longer did walls chop up the area, stifling the natural light. The flow of the area pleased Taylor. As they roamed around downstairs, she couldn't help but think how happy a family could be in the home. It looked great. The interior still held all the charm as before. Now, with modern upgrades, the dwelling was the perfect home.

Taylor signed the papers Brent presented. Not questioning anything, she filled out the lines asking for contact information and extended the clipboard. Pressing her lips together, she kept silent, afraid to trust anything that might escape her mouth. Taylor was scared she might express, consciously or not, the thoughts drifting around in her head.

"This isn't goodbye." Brent moved closer. "There's no reason for it to be." With tenderness, he toyed with a loose curl that had escaped the hair clip she wore. "I'm sure you feel the same way as I do, and if it's meant to be—"

Taylor lifted her hand to his mouth, covering his lips to interrupt his words. "Yes, I'm attracted to you. That's all. It's been nice getting to know you. Please try to understand, though. I'm very involved in my work, and my life in Raleigh is important to me."

He accepted the clipboard from her, leaving any words he wanted to say unspoken. Instead, his lips touched hers in a tender kiss. Then he turned, closing the door behind him. As Taylor rotated the ring on her finger, she wondered if her life was as mapped out as she thought.

CHAPTER EIGHT

"OH, MY, THE ring is more beautiful than I remembered." Kay Harrison trembled as she touched the once-lost treasure that rested on Taylor's finger. Despite her best efforts, a little tear slipped down her cheek. It was a dream come true. The family heirloom was finally home where it belonged. With one look at the ring, Kay knew what she wanted to do with the family's legacy.

Taylor hugged her grandmother. "I'm sorry. I can't get it off my finger. I'll go to the jewelry store during my lunch hour and have the clerk remove it."

The older woman flashed a grin, excited to share her next words. "No, dear, that's not what I want at all. I was planning to give the ring to you anyway. Please keep it. One day, you will have a family and pass it down."

Louise Matthews bustled into the room, carrying a tray of tea.

"Look, Louise. Isn't the stone pretty?"

Setting the tray upon the coffee table, Louise took hold of Taylor's hand, admiring the square nugget perched on a wide, white-gold band. "Yes, it's an amazing ring. I'm glad it's found. I've heard so many stories about this mysterious piece of jewelry."

"You have?"

Louise looked from the band to Taylor and completely changed the subject. "Tell me, Taylor, did Brent do a good job on the renovations?"

"He did a great job, Louise. The place retained its character. Looks fantastic. I brought pictures so you both can see how beautiful the inside turned out. It should be sold in no time. I just wish you would have told me that Brent Roberts was your nephew."

With a sorrowful expression, Louise glanced toward Kay, then again at Taylor. "I'm sorry. We didn't think to say anything at first, and once we discovered you two were dating, we didn't want to cause you to feel pressured by the fact that Brent was my nephew. I hope you'll forgive us."

Kay rushed in, adding, "Is it serious yet? When's your next date?"

The questions shook Taylor, and for some reason she almost blurted a joyful, "Yes!"

Instead, she coolly replied, "We went out only a few times, nothing regular. Ladies, I'm busy at work right now. I don't have any extra time for a serious relationship."

AFTER AN ENJOYABLE day spent with her grandmother, Taylor soaked in a bath. Water pulsated from the jets and swirled around her body. She stretched out her legs in the soaker tub, immersed in bubbles and the scent of lilac from a candle she had lit. As she washed her face, the sapphire sparkled, reflecting off the overhead light. Taylor admired the stone that seemed to demand attention. For a second, the thought flashed in her mind to have it appraised. Deep down, she didn't care what the ring was worth. This was a legacy from her ancestors, and she would wear it with pride. It was irreplaceable.

Pushing herself from the bathtub, she wrapped a towel about her. Anyway, she couldn't get the ring off, an issue she planned to fix as soon as she could take the time. Once the band was free from her finger, she would purchase a nice chain. Then she could wear it around her neck. Taylor sank into her bed and inhaled a breath of comfort. It was good to be home.

TAYLOR'S EYES WHIPPED open. Shock reverberated through her mind as she recalled the vivid dream that woke her. What was going on in her head?

She lay in bed, pulling the covers around her as she ogled the clock perched on top of a night table. Four-thirteen a.m. glowed on the digital dial. Shifting to the side of the bed, Taylor dangled her feet over the edge, the nightmare alive in her mind. Why in the world would she be lost—and in her office, of all places? She shook her head in wonder and relived the seemingly real events.

Looking around in surprise as a feeling of bewilderment closed in. Searching for a way out. She couldn't find the door. Every time she moved, there was another wall in front of her. A part of the office seemed familiar. The rest of the room looked foreign.

Taylor's legs swung as she drifted deep in thought. She didn't understand the frequent dreams. Never had she been one to let her imagination run wild. Why now was her mind conjuring up so many strange things? Five minutes later, still wide awake, she decided to get up and shower. Maybe a cup of flavored coffee and the sunrise would help her feel better. Any hope of sleep was gone, anyway.

SITTING AT THE table, Taylor fiddled with the stone on her finger. She recalled her grandmother's expression as she examined the ring for the first time. The happiness she'd witnessed there was something Taylor couldn't put into words. As the next two hours passed and the sun rose in the sky, Taylor basked in her pride at finding the ring and the joy of being home. Her spirits weren't dampened even by the fact that her grandmother would start going back to church the following Sunday and wanted Taylor to accompany her.

While Taylor had stayed in the Harrison home, she had come to a few conclusions. One, she could indeed take time to do things for herself. Mugful's wouldn't collapse if she took a vacation day. Two, going to church with Granny Kay wasn't supposed to be a burden. Maybe she needed more of God in her life.

If she started to enjoy some down time, maybe she'd be less stressed and would sleep better at night. Today, she planned to relax and enjoy her home again.

After doing some reading, she busied herself with a few chores. First, she grabbed her cleaning supplies and dusted her condominium. Going from one room to another had her amazed. The dust that accumulated over the weeks was astonishing. Sure, she had stopped by her condo occasionally to check her messages from her home phone and retrieve clean clothes. She hadn't taken time to tidy up. As she polished her end tables, a realization entered her mind. No wonder her grandmother always seemed to be busy. She refused to hire anyone to help keep that big place in Liberty

Cove organized. Taylor swiped her hall mirror as a chuckle escaped her lips. *Imagine having to keep that place spotless. No, thank you.*

AFTER INDULGING IN another bubble bath, Taylor put on her favorite nightgown and prepared for bed. Before she tucked in, she stepped inside her walk-in closet, selecting an outfit for her first day back. A small pile of clothes lay tossed on the floor. Taylor eyed the garments then took a moment to stuff them into a laundry bag. On the way to work, she planned on dropping them off at the dry cleaners. She was amazed how things could become neglected in a short time.

Tomorrow would be her first day back on a regular schedule at Mugful's. She didn't even want to guess how many things Dave had left dangling so he could make it home in time for supper. No worries—she was determined to whip her office back in shape in no time.

THE WIND SWIRLED, blowing files all around. It was as if a hurricane had hit her office, debris flying everywhere. Staplers, envelopes, pens whizzed by. The more Taylor picked up sheets of paper, the more additional documents seemed to accumulate. These were important! She couldn't lose them!

Why couldn't she manage to stack them all in a pile? How could they multiply so fast? The phone rang, and she rushed across the room to answer it just as a gust of air blew fierce, grabbing a stack of folders out of her hands. Taylor heard her boss's loud rant coming from the end of the receiver. She didn't know what he was saying, but something was wrong. He was yelling. Then all at once, the sound changed. Brent's smooth baritone voice rang in her ear, asking her if the space looked okay. Was everything the way she wanted it?

Was it...was it...?

Taylor jerked awake and took a shaky breath, rubbing her eyes. Another weird dream. Where were they coming from? Slinging her arm across her forehead, she searched her mind for an explanation. As far back as she could remember she had always slept through the night. What few dreams she did have while sleeping were just fragments of meaningless events that never lasted long. They weren't anything she could remember this well. Looking at the clock, she groaned at the time. She'd gone to bed at twelve. Now it was five-thirty in the morning. Reaching for her pillow, askew on the far side of the bed, she contemplated how the hours had passed so quickly while in her mind the wind blew about, and she'd tracked down endless numbers of reports.

Was her life the same way?

CHAPTER NINE

TAYLOR PARKED HER car and headed for the elevator. Despite the disturbing dream and waking earlier than expected, Taylor was ready to tackle the day. Walking to her corner office, she greeted the receptionist and her assistant. No doubt the day would hold lots of surprises. She was ready. This was her territory. She was ready to tackle any situation that came her way.

At lunchtime, Taylor chose to order a sandwich from the corner deli and remain in her office. It had been a busy morning, riddled with little problems. Although her assistant had done a good job, he had different priorities.

Dave poked his head into the office and dropped off the lunch he had offered to fetch.

Taylor nodded thank-you as she listened to excuses from a supplier who had missed adding one of the stores to the delivery route. A lot of loose ends had to be dealt with today. Taylor was determined to maintain a profit margin, and things like delayed supplies often meant unhappy customers who would shop somewhere else.

AN HOUR BEFORE she planned to leave, Mr. Zimmerman called an impromptu meeting. Taylor breezed into the conference room, glancing at the pictures of the various stores scattered throughout the different states. She claimed a seat then opened her laptop and answered a co-worker's e-mail while she waited for her superior to start the discussions. The day had proven to be full of activity and challenge, and she was happy to be back.

During the gathering, she learned that Mugful's had risen in sales and was nipping at the heels of another major coffee chain. Mr. Zimmerman focused on passing the competition and becoming the largest beverage corporation in the United States.

The president talked of expanding to Central America, where they could hit a major area that he was sure would bring the company to the top. Since the competition had several espresso shops in Panama, he felt that expanding to that region would make the difference. Before he closed the meeting, he expressed to Taylor that he wished to speak with her at a later date about the pending project in the Republic of Panama.

TAYLOR STAYED LATE most days that week, glad to be back at her job.

Today she was almost the last person to leave the office building. On the way home, her mind traveled through her return to her duties at the corporate office of Mugful's.

She was pleased with how things had gone. As far as Taylor was concerned, everything was back to normal. She had cleared up those few situations that caused her to need to work overtime. From here on in, she anticipated more normal working hours, maybe even getting home by six in the evening.

Except, she had to admit, a part of her no longer looked forward to returning to an empty house, and she missed seeing Brent with his breakfast offering every morning.

PROPPED IN HER bed, Taylor was absorbed in her latest novel. She concentrated on the character who had returned home to her family and lost love after an unhappy career in show business.

A song sounded in the room. With her eyes on the pages of her paperback, she reached over and picked up her cell phone. When she heard the voice on the other end, she couldn't help but be captivated by his charming tone. She placed her marker in the pages, laying down the book.

"I hope you don't mind me calling. I tried to contact you earlier, but I didn't get an answer."

Regardless of her hesitancy regarding Brent, she smiled. "No, I don't mind. How has your week gone?"

"It's been busy. I've got a big project close to the hardware store. The owner of the property is turning an unused building into a retail center. My mom is doing much better too. The doctors put her on some new medication that's supposed to help her memory. So did you return to a pile of paperwork and headaches?"

Taylor rested on the pillow, relaxing as they chatted. Listening to the flow of his words, she realized she didn't care what they discussed. The two of them were talking, for now, and that was all that mattered. They could be gabbing about the weather—she didn't care.

"Things at the office weren't as bad as I expected. The manager is talking about expanding to Central America. It'll be a big step for Mugful's."

"An expansion, huh? The company is growing. I still can't believe you work for that yuppie place."

"All right, now. If we were in the same room, I'd throw my pillow at you for that comment."

"If you did, I'd keep it and make you come and try to take it back. I promise I'd pretend to put up a good fight."

For the next hour, they took turns talking, each laughing at various things the other said. Before Brent said goodnight, he asked her if she'd go out to dinner with him on Saturday night. Without considering all those things that gave her doubt, she answered a quick, "Yes. That would be great."

Taylor pressed *end* on the cell phone and snuggled down in the covers. Staring at the ceiling, she nibbled at her lip while reconsidering her rash decision. *Boy, I know how to step in it with both feet. Even if I do like him, the more I see Brent, the closer we grow, the more complicated my life gets.* She turned off the bedside light and lay in scrutiny of her decision and Brent Roberts.

THE NEXT MORNING, Taylor relaxed on the sofa. Without thinking, she opened her phone. Just as she started to punch in the number, she stopped in her tracks, swallowing hard. What in the world was she doing? She was on the verge of calling Brent, for goodness sake. Treading on thin ice. Yeah, she liked the guy and couldn't deny how he made her feel, still…

Tossing the couch pillow to the other end, she voiced her concerns aloud. "What am I going to do about you, Brent Roberts?"

She mulled over the potential problems. This so-called relationship with Brent could turn out to be a big mistake. She was happy and things were good just the way they were. So she was a little lonely at times. Escaping into a good book took care of that, and there was always something to improve with her stores. Never a dull moment at the job, that's for sure.

As she was about to convince herself to call Brent after dinner and tell him she didn't want to see him again, the phone rang. A glance at the number had her blowing out a breath of air in relief.

"Hi, Granny Kay." As the two women talked, Taylor brewed her favorite coffee and perched in front of the big window that overlooked the flower garden. Her grandmother relayed the details of her recent doctor's visit and talked about being able to attend church.

"Do you think it's wise? You need to be careful."

"I know dear, and I will be very cautious. Besides, you will be with me."

Taylor's old habit of trying to find excuses almost had her blurting a copout, and then she remembered that she had promised herself to slow down just a little and pay some attention to her spiritual side. As she was about to speak, her grandmother added, "Remember, dear, you said you would go."

Taylor took a sip from her teal-colored coffee mug. "I did, Granny Kay, and I'll be there bright and early Sunday morning." The conversation ended as both agreed that Taylor would drive her grandmother's car. The sedan was bigger than her little sport compact and made getting in and out easier.

AT SIX, BRENT waited at Taylor's door, more nervous than any date he'd been on. He had stopped by the florist and selected red roses for his date. As the door opened, his worries slipped away and he smiled, handing the flowers to Taylor. "Hi, there. Lovely flowers for a beautiful lady." He extended a small bow.

All day, his thoughts had been on very little except their date. The past weeks had rattled his comfort zone and caused him to rethink his future.

Taylor accepted the flowers, her cheeks tinting pink. "Corny as that sounds, thanks for the roses."

There was something different about Taylor than other woman. Brent couldn't explain it, not even to himself. Nevertheless, the more time he spent with Taylor, the more he sensed deep within that they were meant to be together. No matter what she claimed about her job, she wanted something outside of a lifetime of snuggling with her corporate duties. *Taylor Harrison is afraid of showing a man her vulnerable side.*

Not that he'd ever mind her working, if that was the lifestyle she chose. After all, he admired her commitment to Mugful's. It showed she had staying power.

While the two of them hadn't known each other long, he had started to care about Taylor in a way he never had for any woman before. Oh, initially she seemed a bit stuck-up and bullheaded. The woman was all determination and sheer will. But he had observed the real Taylor Harrison, the one she tried to hide from the world.

Many little things she'd said or done showed him that she was searching for fulfillment in life. The day she stepped up and helped Daisy was an eye-opener. Then, he recollected the time they went shopping for flooring. She'd left him at the counter, finalizing the purchases, and walked to the garden center. When he found her, she was admiring a statue of an angel holding a bird. He didn't think he'd ever forget the look on her face as she admired the simple figurine. So serene, peaceful. Like an angel herself.

Those actions revealed who Taylor Harrison really was. He prayed that she would stop resisting how well they got along together. Maybe, if she did, she would see the possibilities. The fact she lived in Raleigh was nothing of concern—an hour's driving time was the least of his concerns.

TAYLOR HAD TO admit she was impressed. Brent had gone all out. He booked reservations at one of the best restaurants in Raleigh and even wore a suit. During the evening, she laughed at his jokes, relaxing as the date passed. All thoughts of informing him that she didn't want to see him again vanished.

When they returned to her condominium, she invited him inside. The two of them finished off the night sitting together on the sofa, holding hands and embracing. As the evening grew late, she walked Brent to the door.

"Taylor, I've enjoyed the time we've spent together. I want us to see each other regularly and explore where our relationship might go." Then he hugged her with unquestioned affection.

The kiss they shared stirred emotions in Taylor that she remained determined to push aside. Even so, there was something about Brent that beckoned to her heart and her values. As she pulled away, those baby-blue eyes of his turned from a dark, passionate intensity to calm, smoothing shade.

"I don't mind telling you I'm confused. The way I feel about you doesn't change anything. My career comes first. Don't expect a lot right now."

"So you admit you feel something for me?"

She gave him a playful slap. "Goodnight, Brent!"

"Goodnight, Taylor. Sweet dreams."

TAYLOR'S DAYS DRAGGED. Issues with a Mugful's shop in a neighboring city had her rearranging her schedule. During all the hustle, she spoke to Brent only a couple of times.

She finished her work week in exhaustion. She had put in extra hours, conducted three meetings, and was ready for the some time off. Her second week back had proven to be an undertaking. Taylor couldn't wait to spend some quiet, peaceful time alone.

Brent invited her to go to the movies, and she turned him down, explaining she wanted to spend her Saturday evening lounging with a book.

Retiring early with her latest novel was the plan. The apartment was quiet and she snuggled in her queen-size bed, engrossed in reading. The cell phone played a faithful tune from its perch on the side table. Picking it up, she grinned when she saw the number that beamed on the front.

Brent's voice eased from the airwaves. "I don't mean to disturb you. I just wanted to talk. How has your day been?"

"That's okay." Taylor laid the open book down beside her. "I made it a point to rest today. Other than running an errand to the grocery store, I stayed home. What did you do?"

"I went over to Aunt Louise's and planted some new flowers. She and Kay bought some butterfly bushes and didn't want to wait on the boy who mows to plant them, so I helped."

"What would those two ladies do without you around?"

"It's no big deal. I don't mind doing things for them. I'll help you too, if you ever need a gardener or a plumber or maybe a room built onto your condo."

Her laughter rang out. "What in the world would I want with a room built onto my condominium?"

"Just saying…your wishes are my desires, milady."

They chatted on. Taylor talked about the show she watched on television earlier and laughed as Brent mimicked his favorite scene in a comedy he'd recently seen.

The conversation grew serious as each told of aggravations that made the workweek stressful. Taylor snuggled into the covers while listening to the melody of Brent's voice.

Before he ended the phone call, he issued a final comment that would stay in her mind, even if she didn't want to remember the words. "I'm not giving up on you. I know we would be great together, if only you dropped your guard, like today. You know, it's possible to have a career and a relationship. It's something people do every day."

"Not easily, and not without sacrifices."

"Don't you think love is worth the risk?"

"I just don't know."

"I do."

SHE HELD TIGHT to the phone. The sound of his voice radiated through the line as he laughed. His tone turned serious. "We're having a guest speaker at Liberty Cove Worship Center tomorrow. I look forward to hearing his testimony."

"Yes, that's right. I'm going to drive Granny Kay to the service. Would you like to ride with us?"

While they talked, her heart wanted to explode with joy. Never had she felt like this about a man. The scenery changed. At once, she was in the front of Mugful's corporate building. Brent was holding her hand, and they were strolling past the structure. Mr. Zimmerman appeared at the big glass doors. He pushed open the entrance and called out her name. Taylor pulled away from Brent, shaking her head, and rushed toward her boss.

The man laughed menacingly. Scared, she retreated in haste, stepping in Brent's direction.

Then she saw the look of hope on his face.

Both men implored her, reaching out. What should she do? Which way did she want to go?

SUNDAY MORNING, TAYLOR drove to Liberty Cove, thinking about her strange dream. After several good nights' sleep, she had convinced herself that the visions were gone. The last one told a different story. While Taylor drove the miles to Liberty Cove, she tossed about the reasons for the sudden, emotionally taxing nightmare. None came to mind. At least one good thing had happened in the last few days—her grandmother's hip had been pronounced fully healed. No longer did she have to use a wheelchair to get around.

When Taylor arrived at the well-manicured house in Liberty Cove, Louise was still in her robe. She excused herself and returned to bed with a cold. Taylor was about to help her grandmother into the passenger side of the vehicle when a familiar white pick-up truck pulled into the drive and parked beside her compact. In shock, she watched as Brent got out, dressed in a suit and tie.

"I almost didn't make it on time."

Taylor forced her eyes away from the delicious-looking man dressed in the navy ensemble. "Made it for what?"

As if he didn't hear her remark, he greeted Kay with a quick kiss upon her cheek. "Hello, Mrs. Harrison. Taylor called me last night and invited me to ride to church with the two of you."

Kay glanced at her granddaughter, smiling. "That's a nice idea. Brent, you drive. Taylor can ride up front. I'll sit in back. There's as much room back here as the front has. I'm sorry to say Louise is feeling under the weather."

"She is?" Concern etched his voice. His eyes raked over Taylor, admiring her as he sent a wink in her direction. "You ladies excuse me. I'll be right back as soon as I check on Aunt Louise."

Brent walked into the house and left Taylor scratching her head and wondering. Did he say *she* had called him and invited him to church?

DURING THE SERVICE, Brent sat between Taylor and her grandmother. Every so often, he laid his hand on top of Taylor's and shot her his crooked smile.

Taylor reflected his attention with a shaky grin. In a nervous gesture, she crossed her legs. Her mind raced with thoughts. She touched the stone that hung on an eighteen-carat white-gold chain from her neck. What had propelled her to call him and more importantly, *when* did she call him? Why couldn't she recall the phone conversation? Then a faint memory surfaced.

Yes, she remembered talking to him, only in a dream.

Quietly, Taylor reached inside her purse and took a quick peek at the call log on her cell phone. As hard as it was to believe, she *had* called Brent. According to her phone, she'd dialed his number sometime after midnight. She glanced sideways in his direction. Her emotions teetered up and down like child's see-saw ride. Her conception of right and wrong were starting to blend together. Making matters worse, the pastor's sermon was about placing too much focus on the temporary things in this world instead of concentrating on family and eternal life. She bit her lip as Pastor Grant's words dug in. Bible verses he quoted seem to rub her raw, chafing her conscience. She wasn't a bad person. She was entitled to a career as much as the next person. What was so wrong with that?

BACK AT LOUISE'S house, Taylor and Brent helped Kay inside. Louise was up and feeling better. She'd heated a casserole out of the freezer and invited Brent to stay and have lunch. Things were happening too fast—Louise and her grandmother were getting the cozy notion that they were now a steady pair.

Were they?

Maybe... Taylor's lips parted, beaming a wide smile. In her heart, she was glad to be spending the afternoon with him.

THE FOLLOWING MONTH slipped by in a normal routine for Taylor. Despite her uncertainty, she went along with her heart instead of her head and started going out with Brent once a week. Snuggling in his arms gave her a much-needed break from everyday tasks. Matters had improved at work. Her late nights at the office had eased up.

She continued to struggle with strange dreams, although they weren't as frequent as before. She figured she managed four good nights' sleep during the week. For some reason, the dreams always ended with her being pulled out of trouble or saved by Brent. Why, she couldn't figure out. He didn't need to save *her* from anything. As much as she liked Brent and enjoyed the flirtation, a future with him was doubtful. Oh, he seemed responsible and hardworking, but she worried he lacked a certain dedication. Brent never hesitated to change his work schedule if something better came about. Just like that, he would drop everything. Once, he even rescheduled a Friday meeting to bid on a job just to go with the church on a weekend retreat. That she couldn't understand, and she didn't believe it was any way to run a business. Yes, he was successful. Sometimes though, he acted as if his business came second to recreation. To her way of thinking, a person's career should be their top priority.

CHAPTER TEN

EYES STARED BACK at her—cold eyes, circling around, laughing and mocking. Brent moved up and down with the animals as the carousel horses rotated. Her grandmother rode in a bench seat shaped like a fish. She tossed her head back and laughed. Brent waved, signaling her to join them. She didn't budge. Round and round they went, having the time of their life.

Man, she hated that old circus ride—always had. Taylor shook her head and stepped away.

As she sat on the side of her bed, her body slumped—this was a bad way to start a Monday morning. For the umpteenth time in the past few months, Taylor wondered why she was having such odd, annoying dreams. Maybe she needed to see a doctor. Gathering her clothes, she headed for the shower, hoping the day would get better.

TAYLOR WALKED DOWN the hall to her office. She smiled as she greeted her assistant. Dave wasn't such a bad guy to employ, and he was improving. He managed to accomplish his tasks, even if he did hate to work late. Taylor had a meeting at two with the president of the company. Although she couldn't imagine what it was about, she wasn't concerned. Mr. Zimmerman often called unexpected meetings, just to keep tabs on the corporation's branches. However, Taylor had stayed up late double-checking the figures, aware he would ask her to recap the profit margin of her region.

THAT AFTERNOON, TAYLOR sat across the table from Mr. Zimmerman and listened to his proposal and plans. He hadn't even asked to see the figures for the satellite offices. Her boss was absorbed in his own statistics and propositions for expansion. A decision on her part loomed in the air.

"Taylor, I'm pleased with your work and the dedication you have shown this company. A manager in Virginia has shown an interest in this move, but you've been with Mugful's longer, so I'm giving you first chance. I feel it's important to expand outside the United States, and I want to assign my best. I have confidence that you'll put forth every effort to make the upcoming coffee bistro in Panama a success. This position is yours if you want it. I do need you to give me an answer by the end of the week. As I said, if you don't want this opportunity, then Avery Thomas is more than willing to go."

PANAMA. WHAT WAS she going to do? All the way home, she debated. Excitement swept through her bones, tingled along her spine. Mr. Zimmerman had confided that she was his top producer and the one he preferred to oversee the expansion. This was what she had worked for—proof that she was on her way to the top in the company. Her boss even hinted that one day soon the position of Vice President of Operations would become available—and the person who made a success out of this venture would likely be the best candidate for the position.

Three years. That was how long Mr. Zimmerman needed someone to stay in Panama. Taylor would be responsible for setting up contacts to keep the beverage shop running. She'd also need to do a lot of marketing. Mr. Zimmerman had already rented an office, and a temporary job service had lined up applicants to be interviewed for the administrative assistant position. Contractors were in place to start redesigning the shop in downtown Panama.

If all went smoothly, it would be ready to open for business within six months. Someone needed to be available in that area pronto to search for a manager, hire the staff, and oversee matters.

Was she that someone?

She unlocked her front door and laid down her briefcase. Taylor had a mere week to make up her mind. The company planned to have someone in place by next month. If she passed on this opportunity, it would go to the next in line. Did she want to give away her chance to reach the top at Mugful's Corporation? After all, what would her life amount to if she couldn't move up in her profession?

The phone rang, interrupting her thoughts.

"I'm coming into Raleigh on Wednesday. Can we have lunch?"

Taylor's mind was so immersed in the new developments at Mugful's, she responded without giving Brent's question much consideration. "Yes, sure, that will be okay. I'll see you then."

He hesitated. "I'll meet you in front of your office building. Are you okay?"

"Sure. Never better. See you Wednesday."

TAYLOR HAD GIVEN her decision to Mr. Zimmerman after spending the last two days deliberating. While part of her, deep down, did not want to make the move, she would be a fool not to jump at the opportunity. This was a once-in-a-lifetime chance. She stepped outside the corporate building just in time for Brent's vehicle to pull to the curb.

Brent jumped out to greet her. Without hesitating, he embraced in a hug and kissed her cheek before opening the truck door. Grinning, he assisted her as she struggled into the pick-up in her two-piece suit.

As he settled into the driver seat, he smiled. "It's good to see you. I know we had a date last week, but I've missed you."

Forcing a smile, Taylor made polite sounds as Brent talked, her mind focusing on what she needed to do next. The hard part lay ahead. Somehow, she had to tell Brent—and worse, her grandmother—about the changes that were going to take place in her life. Though she liked Brent, she had no choice. He wasn't the problem, she would tell him. After all, they had just started to form a close relationship. Finding a way to explain to Granny Kay would be torture.

AT THE RESTAURANT, Brent seized her hand and led her into the dining area. After they ordered, he gazed at Taylor. "What's going on? I sense you have something on your mind. You're much quieter than usual."

"Well…this isn't easy." Straightening her back, she removed her hands from the top of the table, placing them in her lap. It was now or never. This was why she held her emotions back from Brent.

Somehow, she sensed things were going to change between them forever because she'd accepted this position. "I've been offered an opportunity I can't refuse. This would be a major step toward a huge promotion at Mugful's. My boss has asked me to relocate to Panama for three years and supervise the growth of a chain of coffee shops there."

Taking a sip of his beverage, Brent hesitated before he spoke. He'd truly believed they were growing closer...or had it just been a fantasy? He hoped someday they would have a future together. Now, she was moving—thousands of miles away, to another country.

"Well, if that is what you want, then I suppose you need to go...of course, *I* don't want you to go. I was hoping we were moving toward something permanent." Brent leaned forward. "I'll be praying about this new turn of events with your job and our relationship."

Her eyes grew a shade darker. The way she stared at him, hard and unyielding, convinced him to change the track of the conversation. Brent didn't want to alienate her. He understood how life could often take surprise turns. He wasn't about to do anything to put a wall between them. "What does Kay think about it?"

Putting down her fork, she heaved a breath and eyed him. "Well..." She looked away then back at him again. "If things were different... I'm sorry. It's just...I've worked too hard not to reap the rewards."

"I understand. Was Kay all right when you told her?" he asked again.

"She doesn't know yet. I'm going to church with her on Sunday, and I'll tell her afterward. Brent, I want you to know I do like you—a lot. It just doesn't change the facts. I told you from the get-go that my job comes first. I can't turn down this chance. In three years, I will be back. I'm not saying you should wait around, but if you're single then, maybe we'll resume seeing each other."

Throughout the rest of lunch, Taylor did most of the talking. She engaged in idle chit-chat, filling him in on the plans for the temporary move. Brent offered an occasional remark, but for the most part, he just sat and listened. He was deflated, as if someone had stuck a pin in his balloon and popped it. He couldn't think. The words from Taylor's lips stung, like being attacked by dozens of bees, and his emotions dulled. The sharp bitterness of the moment stabbed into the very midst of his soul. The rest of their lunch turned into a blur.

BRENT PULLED TO the curb in front of Taylor's office building. He reached for her and drew her close. Holding her, he trailed a line of kisses from her neck to her lips. He hoped his embrace would leave her with no question as to how important she'd become to him.

Regardless, he wouldn't issue forth any protests. Taylor had to be happy and if this job offer pleased her, then he couldn't stand in the way. He would wait on God and His guidance. *I haven't made it this far without realizing man's plans can be turned topsy-turvy if God has a different path for us to follow.*

THE SUNDAY MORNING Taylor dreaded had come. She couldn't keep her attention on the service. As she sat between her grandmother and Louise, she chaffed at Brent's presence. She had forgotten she would also see him. Of course, he would sit close to his aunt. Taylor fiddled with the ring that dangled around her neck. Even though the situation was uncomfortable, she soaked in the closeness of both her grandmother and Brent. This would be one of the last times she would sit beside them.

Brent sneaked glances in her direction. Taylor found herself wishing she could read his mind. Although, it didn't matter—she had to do what was necessary.

As the sermon proceeded, her mind raked over her intentions to visit her grandmother every two months once the new Mugful's opened.

Taylor's attention jumped from her plans to listening to Pastor Grant as he preached on Jesus and the Sermon on the Mount. Brent whispered to his aunt and she gazed at his warm image from the side. *If things were different, something good might have developed...* Nevertheless, there was nothing to do about the situation. A new beginning waited.

AFTER THE SERVICE, the older ladies invited Brent to join them for lunch. He declined, claiming he had to do something important. He hugged Taylor and she whispered in his ear. "Thank you, Brent. You're a great guy."

Before he turned her loose, he held her hand and mumbled, "Yeah...where has that gotten me?"

"Oh, stop." She play-smacked him.

He turned serious. "You know you can call me anytime. I care about you very much." With a quick kiss on the cheek, he left.

LUNCH WITH THE ladies had Taylor laughing. The older women always seemed to have some amusing tale to regale her with. When the humor wore off, they inquired about her work, and she had to remind herself to keep quiet—at least for a little while longer. Taylor wanted to be alone with Granny Kay when she told her the news.

After the meal, she helped Louise clear the table. "I'm going to take Granny Kay out to the patio. I have something important to discuss with her."

Louise eyed Taylor, picking up on the serious tone in her voice. "Is everything okay?"

"Yes, fine. There has been a change at work that affects me. I need to tell Granny Kay about it first. Just promise me you will always be here for her and you'll let me know if she needs anything."

Louise watched Taylor walk away and wondered what was going on.

AFTER TAYLOR EXHAUSTED every possible way to explain to Granny Kay why she felt the need to move to Central America, she gave up trying to reason and reached for her grandmother's wrinkled hand.

The older woman's eyes gathered tears. The lines on her face etched more prevalent as color drained from her cheeks.

"Granny Kay, will you say something?" Taylor squeezed her fingers.

Silence filled the air for what seemed like eternity. Granny Kay raised her head higher, as if she were heaving up a heavy boulder. "Taylor, why?"

"I've explained why. Please try to understand." As badly as Taylor wanted to drop the subject, she owed her grandmother as much. How could she convince her that while this move was just temporary, it would pave her future? "You know how hard I've worked to move up in the company. This opportunity will make it possible for me to transfer to a higher position one day."

Wiping a tear that escaped down her own face, Taylor looped her arm around her grandmother's shoulders. "It's just for three years. I'll visit every couple months and we can talk on the phone every week."

The older lady patted Taylor's hand and stood. With her back turned, she spoke. "I love you. I'm going to miss you. Even if we can talk every week, it won't be the same as having you an hour's drive away."

Taylor rose and clutched her grandmother's hand again. Without saying a word, she led her grandmother to the front door and kissed her on the cheek. The hug that followed was long and sorrowful. Taylor planned to make the most of the hugs before she had to leave.

TAYLOR'S DRIVE HOME was a blur of tears and sobbing. Leaving Granny Kay unhappy had been the hardest thing she had done in ages.

Unlocking the door to her place, Taylor hurried inside and shut herself away from the world. Making her way to the bathroom, she stared long and hard into the mirror at the reflection. "Happy now?"

She rubbed the stone to the ring and wondered how she'd even arrived home safely. All she remembered was the bout of crying that overcame her as she backed out of Granny Kay's driveway.

TAYLOR COULDN'T BELIEVE her eyes. Brent stood in front of the entrance to her work building. In his expression, she encountered worry and concern.

"Are you okay?" Tenderness sounded from his voice.

"I'm fine. What are you doing here?"

His gaze narrowed with concern. "You called me last night and asked me to come. You said we needed to talk. What's up?"

Twisting her mouth, she brought her cup of cappuccino close. *It wasn't just a dream.* She'd called him in her sleep again. A flashback hit her. She was running down a long hallway of what appeared to be a plane. She punched his number and begged him to come.

Oh, what a fool she was.

Taylor tried to recap some of the unclear details. All Taylor remembered was saying she'd made a mistake and wanted to talk.

She blew a hard breath from her lungs. Man, she must be nuts. Certifiable. Oh yes, the sooner she got away, the better. Never in her life had she talked in her sleep or battled with such weird, vivid dreams. And sleep *phoning*? Not until she met this man.

Things had to change and soon.

Closing her eyes for a second, she gathered momentum to speak. "Brent, look…I'm sorry to bring you all this way for nothing. I don't remember why I called you. I can assure you everything's fine. My itinerary is the same. I'll be leaving soon. I was tired last night and really, I don't know why I said those things. Just leave and forget about it."

That was it. She spoke the royal proclamation and then trotted into the foyer of the corporate building.

"Taylor, wait!"

Brent raised his voice, but it was too late—either she didn't hear him or didn't want to acknowledge his plea. The elevator doors shut, closing on his hopes for the future.

Brent hung his head and walked outside to the truck. As he pulled into the heavy traffic of Raleigh, he took a quick look at the clouds. "Lord, You know I love Taylor. I think she could love me, if only she'd let her guard down. She's scared. She thinks her life can't include both a marriage and a career. If she's the lady I'm going to spend the rest of my life with, I need Your help. If Taylor Harrison isn't the mate You've picked out for me, please make the hurt go away."

THE WEEKS RACED by. Taylor spent as much time as possible with her grandmother. She managed to speak with her parents, who were on an expedition in Asia. Pride embraced their reactions and warmed Taylor's heart. Theirs were her first sincere congratulations on the new position.

After they offered their best wishes, they informed Taylor that perhaps they would visit during the Christmas holiday, maybe even sooner. Apparently, visiting their daughter abroad held more appeal than seeing her at home.

The night before her plane was to leave, Taylor stood on Louise's porch, waiting for her grandmother to open the door. Brent had invited his aunt for dinner, so she and Kay could have a nice meal alone together.

KAY WOBBLED TO the front hall and invited her granddaughter inside. She clasped Taylor tightly in her arms and squeezed her granddaughter as if eternity revolved around the embrace. Silently, she motioned for Taylor to enter.

"Granny Kay, are you feeling okay? You look a little pale."

The older woman smoothed back her hair and turned her lips up in an attempt to grin. "I'm fine, dear...just a bit down. I guess I'm missing you already."

Over the next couple hours, the women talked and reminisced, trying to pretend that this wasn't Taylor's going away dinner. Taylor giggled as Kay entertained her with stories of some childhood stunts she had pulled.

"Oh, Granny Kay, I love you. We've always been close. Just because I'm going to be in Panama isn't going to change that. I'm only a phone call away."

At nine, after many hugs and tears, Taylor walked out the door. She slid into her car, cranked the keys in the engine, and sat in the driveway. She took a long gaze at the house, watching as her grandmother turned off the porch light. Out of habit, she grabbed hold of the sapphire ring that swung from the chain around her neck, speaking aloud in the soundless car. "Lord, please watch over Granny Kay. You know I love her. Keep her safe until I come home for good."

CHAPTER ELEVEN

Taylor's first couple weeks in Panama City proved a whirlwind. Her days were busy as she searched out distributors and potential employees. The evenings she spent sightseeing, armed with tourist brochures she had picked up at the visitor center.

Taylor figured if Central America was going to be her home away from home for the next few years, she would start by seeing the tourist attractions, then work her way up to growing accustomed to the lifestyle of the Panamanians. Starting over in an exotic new country was exciting. An adventure, really.

Taylor took in large two and three-story houses laced with flowerpots that hung from the sides. The structures around the square were a mixture of Spanish colonial and French. Walking the streets, she studied the buildings, amazed at the beautiful architecture.

Thoughts of Brent soared into her mind. How nice it would be to share this magnificent construction and stonework with him.

But he wasn't there. Never would be.

Under her breath, she scolded herself for allowing the memory of him to taunt her. This was her life for the next few years. The one she had chosen. Brent was over a thousand miles away. That was that. End of the story.

Cocking her head, Taylor stepped up to the entrance of the Canal Museum, determined to put her worries in North Carolina behind her.

BY THE END of the week, Taylor had interviewed several women and hired a receptionist. The woman she chose was experienced and a go-getter, ready to tackle anything.

That evening, after she locked the office doors, she wandered around the streets and checked out some local restaurants. She moseyed into one of the more popular specialty cafés located in the city, purchased an espresso, and seated herself at a table. It never hurt to check out the local competition. As she sipped the poorly brewed beverage, all she could think of was Brent's reaction to her espresso.

MONDAY MORNING, TAYLOR stretched her face toward the sky, peeking through her sunglasses to the top of the high-rise buildings. Never could she remember seeing such giant office buildings or being immersed in so many smells. The Republic of Panama was far more aromatic the United States. Oh yes, Central America had its uniqueness, its advantages. This job of hers was an experience.

With her order of chicken curry from the corner deli, she rushed back to her office. The eight-hundred-square-foot area stood two streets over from the Plaza de Independencia. The location made for an easy commute to the newest addition of a Mugful's café.

Taylor nodded at an older woman walking past her on the sidewalk. Since she moved here, her attitude had softened. The years she'd spent in the corporate world had toughened her. She often sought to create the image of being untouchable toward co-workers and clients, never wanting to mix business with pleasure, not even for a quick lunch. The only exceptions were office parties—those she saw as part of her work duties.

Here, life was different. The short time she'd been in The Republic of Panama already had her greeting strangers and enjoying idle chit-chat with employees. Without thinking, she reached up and touched the ring her grandmother had given her. If only Granny were here, life would be perfect.

And Brent?

Stomping out that thought, she stepped inside her new building and took the elevator to Mugful's Panama headquarters.

The small corner space boasted a reception area and two offices on each side of a long hallway. The passageway in between housed a large counter holding a cappuccino machine. Below the surface stood an under-the-cabinet cooler with snacks.

Taylor greeted her assistant, who sat at the modern glass desk. Brenda Stone was a nice lady with a blissful manner, who moved to Panama seven years ago when her husband accepted a transfer. On the first interview Taylor had with Brenda, she liked her. Maybe it was the fact that the two had a common bond. When they talked, their conversation always drifted to the normal things found in the States. Brenda appeared to have adjusted to life in Central America, even if the woman enjoyed frequently talking about "back home," as she called it.

Taylor couldn't put her finger on the reason, but having Brenda around was like the calm before the storm. The pudgy little woman with a peaceful demeanor not only had dedication, but she also felt like a friend. While Taylor usually made it a policy to keep a professional distance from the people she worked with, the last couple months had been different. As if the social butterfly in her was emerging. Was it Panama…or had watching Brent in his day-to-day activities sparked the change? Taylor smiled at the thought. Despite his frequently unprofessional attitude toward work, he had a welcoming way about him, and people responded positively to his open nature. The people around Panama City were a little like that. They didn't mind speaking their opinions and expected others to be the same.

"Any messages, Brenda?"

"Just one. It's on your desk. Trying that new restaurant I suggested?"

"Thanks. I am. But I feel guilty not bringing you anything."

"Oh no. Slimfast for me."

Laughter filled the office. "Brenda, I think you're just fine the way you are. You don't need to drink a diet shake every day at lunch."

The phone rang and intercepted Brenda's comment. In a hurry, she shook her finger at Taylor. "We can't all be naturally skinny like you, young lady. Some of us have to work at it."

Taylor retreated to her office, and while she ate her lunch, she reminisced about the day she hired Brenda.

She didn't know why she'd found herself asking her jovial secretary to call her by her first name before the interview finished. Since then, she and Brenda interacted not only about business, but also personally, even confiding tidbits of their lives to one another. Somehow, Taylor felt as if she had known Brenda for years.

Her assistant broke into her thoughts as she popped her head in the door. "Don't forget your conference call to Mr. Zimmerman. It's in a few minutes."

"Thanks for reminding me. I've been off my routine this morning."

Brenda took that as an invitation to breeze into the room and adjust the curtains. "Did you have another upsetting night?"

Taylor paused mid-bite. "Yes, I did. I should be getting somewhat used to it. For months now, I've had the same weird dreams at least three times a week." Not wanting to talk about Brent, she waved her hand in the air to dismiss the subject as unimportant. "We'll talk later. I'd better make my call to the States."

AN HOUR LATER, after filling Mr. Zimmerman in on all the happenings of the newest addition to the Mugful's Corporation, Taylor leaned back in her chair. Overseeing the grand opening was exciting, in spite of the issues they'd encountered with the building construction. Thank goodness everything was now on schedule. The event would take place in two months.

Taylor fiddled with a piece of her hair, tucking the fallen lock back into the clip it had escaped from. Out of the blue, a reflection of Brent surfaced.

She was determined the change of scenery here would clear her mind and put her priorities back on track. It wasn't like her to spend so much time thinking about a man. Even the guy she'd almost married hadn't monopolized her thoughts the way Brent did. Taylor's concentration traveled back to the prior night. In her dream, Louise was crying and saying something about Granny Kay. Then the picture changed and she saw her father's face. She couldn't understand what was said, but something was wrong. Just as quickly as the dream started, it ended.

Earlier in the week, her dreams had shifted between her grandmother and Brent. What was going on? The unwarranted fantasies certainly were odd, plaguing her far into the day. Her grandmother had once told her that dreams often told a person important things, if one paid attention.

Walking to the picture window, Taylor gazed out, rubbing away the cold chills that formed on her arms. Were the strange nightmares trying to say more than she wanted to know? Speaking to no one, she voiced her thoughts. "Some things we're better off not knowing." No, she would embrace her future at Mugful's and make the best of this occasion that provided her with a new challenge. After all, lots of other employees would give their eyeteeth to trade places with her. Avery Thomas, Mr. Zimmerman's other choice, had even called before she left North Carolina, assuring her that if she didn't want to make the temporary move, he and his wife would love the chance to experience a few years away from the States.

As she toyed with the sapphire ring, her feelings shifted to her grandmother. She imagined her sitting in her favorite chair, drinking a glass of tea. Maybe she was starting to miss home a bit now that the newness of Panama was wearing off.

Turning back to her desk, she promised herself to call when the work day was finished. Taylor wanted to talk and not be interrupted by her daily activities.

"KAY, YOU LOOK a bit peaked today. Did you rest well last night?" Louise made a path to the door to retrieve the morning paper.

Kay stood staring out the window as if she was waiting for something. Or someone. "I woke early and couldn't get back to sleep." Kay turned and moseyed toward the kitchen. "I may as well make a pot of coffee."

In the kitchen, Louise regarded Kay with uncertainty. Her hobble from the broken hip was no longer prevalent, and Kay's physical health was restored to normal. But Kay had said little about the move Taylor had made. She watched Kay spoon grounds into the coffee pot.

In all the years Louise had known Kay Harrison, the woman was a rock. Nothing shook the faith she held tight to. Taylor's absence, though, had created a weak spot in her friend's blanket of faith.

"Kay, you have to accept Taylor's choice. Leave it in God's hands. The Lord will work everything out."

Kay took a seat at the table, tossing an unsure look toward Louise. "I'm aware of the things I can't change. But Louise, my flesh wants to rise up and be mad. Maybe I'm upset at God for letting her go."

Louise sat across from her pal and unfolded the morning paper. "Nevertheless, you have to remember that the Lord works in ways we can't understand. He knows why this is happening." Louise filled two mugs with hot coffee. "If we keep the faith and continue praying, God will hear us."

Kay murmured something and then sighed. "Sometimes I have my own little pity party, despite my faith. No one knows any better than I do that God will make a way. I have learned through the years that patience is necessary. I know if our prayer lines up with God's will, then things work out."

She lifted her chin and reached for the cup Louise offered. "I remember one time when Taylor was a teenager. She asked how anyone could figure out God's will for their life. I told her that the Bible tells us what He desires us to be—as long as we work toward being the Christian we should be, we accomplish His will. Whatever we do from that point on is meant to glorify God. If we continue to grow toward our relationship with the Lord, then we have Him with us in all we do."

"That's correct. And if God is in our hearts, He'll speak to us."

With finality in her voice, Kay squared her shoulders and sipped her coffee. "Yes, you're right. That's enough of me feeling sorry. I had a long talk with the Lord this morning and was even able to kneel down and pray. I know in my heart Taylor will return, and I won't have to wait three years. I also believe that she and Brent will be together. That boy will be my grandson-in-law one day, and I won't believe anything less."

Kay looked at Louise and chuckled.

"Oh, yes, dear. I too plan on praying every day for her to come home and slow her life down."

Kay rose out of her seat and placed her cup in the sink. "And to marry Brent."

"And to marry Brent. Though, I don't think he's exactly proposed yet."

"Nonetheless, I'm already thinking of name suggestions for my great-grandchildren."

Laughter filled the small kitchen.

THE TELEPHONE RANG. Kay hurried, fast as she could manage, across the room to answer, sure the call was her granddaughter. A rush of nausea swept over her. Today, she'd felt a little off. She'd suffered a spell of sickness earlier in the morning and had spent most of the afternoon resting. Perhaps Taylor's call would make her feel better. Each day she waited and kept her faith that God had a plan to bring her granddaughter home where she belonged.

CHAPTER TWELVE

TAYLOR CUDDLED ON the sofa, enjoying the chat with her grandmother, though the tone in the older woman's voice worried her. Taylor sensed something was off. "Granny Kay, you don't sound like yourself today."

"I'm fine. I just felt a little nauseated this morning. It might be something I ate. Perhaps a virus." Lightening her tone, Kay continued. "I could say the same about you, Taylor dear. My mind may be old, but no less keen. Something is burdening you."

Taylor stretched out her legs. "Why would you say that? I like Panama."

"You don't sound at all like your old self. I know when something's amiss in my granddaughter's life."

Leaning her head against the sofa, Taylor pushed the hair away from her face. "It's nothing…just that I haven't been sleeping very well. It started months ago. I have some of the oddest dreams. Most times, I don't understand at all what they mean."

"Hun, remember what I told you about dreams? They can't always be explained. Sometimes, those fantasies don't mean anything. But other times, those illusions can mean something is bothering us, sparking a battle within our conscience. They may be nothing, but they may be something—especially if they keep reoccurring. You subconscious may be trying to tell you something. Think in context of your life. Don't dismiss dreams so easily. Above all, you must be honest with yourself. Often we have nightmares when we sleep because we lie to ourselves about things."

Before Taylor ended the chat, she promised to visit as soon as the grand opening of Mugful's was complete. In three months, she would fly back to the States for a few days and ensure her grandmother's spirits were raised. She worried her grandmother was letting her health slide, maybe because she missed her.

THE LAST CHAPTER of her latest novel was read. Closing the book, satisfied at the ending, she turned out the light, snuggled into the covers, and drifted off to sleep.

Taylor tossed in the bed as images hovered in her mind. Just before she drifted off, she reached to the bedside table for her phone. Clutching it like a teddy bear, she let sleep claim her...

She counted the number of times the phone rang. A hello expressed with grogginess was replaced by a happy greeting. Harmony in her ears. A melody, the most wonderful, beautiful music she'd heard in a long time. Grinning to herself, she felt giddy, like a teenager again. It was good talking to Brent. She was glad he wasn't mad. Taylor had been afraid he would hang up the telephone—instead, his speech rang out with pleasure.

Deep down, she hoped he didn't meet anyone soon. Never had she felt as connected to anyone as she did to Brent Roberts.

"Taylor, it's good to hear your voice. How are things in Panama?"

"Everything is going as scheduled. Soon the new Mugful's will open. Central America is a wonderful place. The buildings are huge in the city. And so many different structures. The place has everything from colonial era to grass-roofed huts lining the countryside. The water is crystal clear. I wish you were here to see it all."

"It sounds nice, Taylor. I would love to be there too... with you."

When she said goodbye, he bid her to let him call her in Central America once in a while. Automatically, Taylor said yes. When she pressed *end* and heard the silence, her heart ached as if someone were tearing it from her chest. She longed to feel his muscular arms around her. Taylor wanted nothing more at that moment than to be with him, back in the kitchen of her grandmother's home in Liberty Cove, North Carolina.

TAYLOR FUMBLED FOR the blaring alarm and shut off the noise. She grunted and stretched her arms over her head. With her eyes closed, she inhaled a soft breath. As she rose, she sighed. *Man, I feel good this morning. So relaxed.*

She remembered parts of a dream she'd had. Even though large fragments of the conversation were hazy, her mind replayed bits. In the fantasy, she had talked to Brent. Part of her wished it were true. Deep down, she liked the man. No, if she was honest, she was more than fond of Brent Roberts—falling in love with him would be very easy, if she let herself.

Shrugging, she chewed her lower lip as her mind continued to wander. She was far away and Brent couldn't fit into her life right now, no matter how much she wished otherwise. Taylor picked up a picture of her and Granny Kay sitting on her grandmother's porch. As if speaking to her grandmother, she voiced the words, "Naw, things are hectic, Granny Kay. I couldn't give him hope of anything more than a friendship. Maybe in three years…if some lucky woman hasn't snatched him up by then."

"Good morning, Taylor. You look rested today."

Taylor sashayed in the main reception area. "Hi, Brenda. I do feel rested. I had a good night."

"That's good to hear." A smile stretched across Brenda's face. "I have a fresh pot of Mugful's famous brand ready for you. I'm trying all the flavors, so I know what each one tastes like." Her secretary held up an oversized mug to prove her point. "I guess that means you weren't bothered with any crazy nightmares."

Taylor laughed, bee-lining to the decorative office cups. "Oh, you could say just the opposite." Taylor regarded the woman who always had a grin to offer. Curiosity shined on her face.

"I did have a dream, and it was good. At least, I felt satisfied this morning when I woke." In a gesture to share a toast with her cup of espresso, Taylor raised it toward her assistant. "This time, I called Brent and we chatted. The parts I can recall seem real, as if they truly happened." Taking a sip of the hot liquid, she added, "I must admit the prospect of talking to him appeals to me."

Brenda paused with her cup close to her lips. "You could call him anytime, I'm sure. There's nothing wrong with maintaining a friendship with this guy. Who knows? Maybe he'll still be unattached in three years."

Taylor exhaled a lungful of air and searched the room for something to focus on. She didn't like the feeling that suddenly clouded over her.

"I wouldn't feel right stringing him on like that. I figured, at first, I just wanted his friendship. To be honest, I don't think I would be a very good buddy. He's too easy to fall in love with. Brent deserves a woman he can have a normal relationship with. Not a pal. Not me."

As if a boulder had dropped on the building, her spirits plummeted. Nerves danced up and down her spine. For the first time, she found herself wanting much more than comradeship. Her previous close contact with him had left her starved for more. No matter what she said or reasoned, she wanted to go home. To be in love with Brent. But these things were beyond her control.

THE NEXT WEEK whizzed by. Saturday came and Taylor journeyed out to do some more exploring. She dressed in comfortable walking shoes, anxious to familiarize herself with Central America. After all, it was her home for the next three years.

Taylor strolled down the busy streets and listened to the combination of Spanish and English languages surrounding her. She ambled her way to the outskirts of the city where the tropical forest surrounded the Canal.

She visited the Summit Botanical Gardens and Zoo, roaming the pathways and enjoying the orchids. Reading a sign that stood over a particular area of flowers, Taylor read the words out loud. *"Flor del Espirito Santo* orchid. This plant is also known as the Holy Ghost Orchid."

As she traveled through the gardens, she was amazed at the all the foliage. She glanced at the informational tract she held in her hand, noting it said the vegetation totaled over fifteen thousand species of flora. She sipped on her bottled water and read the pages, engrossed in the many interesting sights.

Next, she explored the zoo. She couldn't stop the memories from flooding back, taking her to a time when her grandparents had treated her to a day at a wildlife park. The big stuffed teddy bear she had begged her grandmother to buy in the gift shop still stood in the corner of her bedroom. Everywhere she went, even across the ocean, she found things that reminded her of the kindness and love of Kay Harrison. Hurrying along, she smiled. Yes, she and her grandmother had a tight bond that forged them together.

EXHAUSTED, TAYLOR WALKED into her executive apartment Mugful's provided. As she plopped down on the sofa and removed her tennis shoes, she surveyed the area. Taylor had to admit it was grand. She always prided herself on having a modern condominium and the latest furnishings, but as much as she loved her home and kept in up to date, it certainly wasn't as outstanding as this place. A massive television hung on the far wall. The two bathrooms were floor-to-ceiling marble. Everything in the suite represented luxury and opulence.

Taylor approached the huge windows. For her, the attraction of the eighteenth floor was the stunning view of the city and neighboring waters. In the evening hours, it was a magnificent sight, a background that would relax anyone after a long day.

She reached in her pocket and removed her cell phone. Then, on her way out to the veranda, she snatched a cola from the refrigerator. Nothing like spending a little time stretched out in a chaise lounge, watching the stars. Glancing at the clock on the wall, she thought of Liberty Cove. Her grandmother would be getting ready for bed soon. Taylor ambled outside to enjoy the cool breeze, sip her soda, and call her favorite relative. "Granny Kay, how are you?"

"I'm feeling much better. How are you doing, dear?"

They discussed Kay Harrison's recent doctor visit. Kay chattered on about the unusual weather in North Carolina and her latest church social. Then the older woman asked Taylor about Central America.

"It's a beautiful place. I went sightseeing and took some pictures for you and Louise. I was overwhelmed by its beauty when I first arrived, but one thing I have discovered is that I prefer North Carolina. Panama is wonderful, it's just… the location will never take the place of the United States." Taylor took a drink from the can. "I am going to have a once-in-a-lifetime experience here, that's for sure. But, I'm certain now, North Carolina will always be home to me." Before she ended the conversation, she asked about the Harrison family house.

"No, I haven't sold it yet, dear. Why do you ask?"

"No reason. I was just wondering if anyone bought it. Brent did a wonderful job. I don't think it will be on the market long before some couple snatches it up."

"Yes, you're right. He did a great job. Louise and I went by there the other day. I saw the space. It looked so modern." Before the conversation ended, Kay made an unexpected comment. "It's nice that you and Brent are talking. He was afraid you wanted him out of your life forever. He was glad you called."

Before Taylor had a chance to respond, Kay rushed in with a loud yawn. "Oh, dear, I must go. I'm exhausted, hun. I love you."

Taylor looked at her cell phone in shock. The words she was planning to say before her grandmother ended the call buzzed around in her head—a phone call? Did that dream actually happen?

Leaning her forehead in her hand, she questioned herself. *Did I do something stupid again?*

Before she could come up with an answer her favorite coastal tune sung out in the air. Catching her off guard, the noise made her jump. She turned the phone over and looked at the number, lifting a brow. She was about to find out the answer.

LOUISE WALKED BY Kay in the hall as she retreated to the bedroom. "You seem more relaxed. I guess that means you and Taylor had a good conversation."

"Yes, we did. She told me a bit about Central America. Said she was going to send us pictures of all the charming places. I'm glad she's enjoying the scenery. I'll be even more delighted when she's home."

"That's nice."

Kay changed the subject to the matter weighing on her mind. "Tomorrow morning, I'm going to call that realtor. I haven't signed the contract yet. I believe I should wait awhile before I do."

"Did Taylor say something to change your mind?"

"No, rather, it's the things she left unsaid and a feeling I have. God is telling me something else."

"HELLO, TAYLOR, HOPE I didn't call too late. Taylor, did you hear me? How was your day?"

Taylor glanced at her wristwatch as she relished the smooth-sounding voice on the other end. Her mind itched to ask about the phone call a few days before. If she did, she'd make a fool of herself. She was determined not to come straight out with her concerns. No, she didn't want Brent thinking she had some kind of problem. At least, she didn't use to, not until he came into her life and made her question things she thought she had figured out, like her desires.

"It's not late. I walked around today, visited the zoo and some beautiful gardens. The foliage around the Canal is lovely. Central America is a place everyone needs to visit at least once. The architecture here is amazing. You would appreciate the way these building were crafted."

"Yeah, I bet they are something to look at. Just listening to you the other night intrigued me. I even surfed around on the Internet to get some information and found a few pictures of the area."

"Brent…about that…I hope I didn't disturb you. I…don't guess I realized the time." She squeezed her lips together and then breathed out in exasperation. "I guess I just needed to talk."

"I haven't given up on us. I want us to work on having a relationship one day. With you being over a thousand miles away, it won't be easy, but who knows God's plans? I care for you, more than I can explain right now. If, for the time being, all we can do is make phone calls and maybe see each other when you fly home for a visit, I have to accept things that way."

"I don't know… Why don't you tell me about your day?"

Taylor rose and walked inside, tossing her soda can in the trash pail. Despite her uncertainty, she was once again happy to talk to Brent. As he spoke about his day, she searched for the answer to one annoying question. Why now, at this time in her life, did she have to start falling head over heels for this man?

TAYLOR CLOSED HER phone and retired to the master suite. The words Brent said flew through her head in various directions, like sparklers on the Fourth of July. His declarations of the feelings he had for her glowed, igniting sensations from deep within her soul.

She should be honest with herself. Never in her life had she cared for someone the way she did for him. Brent Roberts was different than any other man she had been involved with. Was he right? Did God have a plan she didn't know about?

As she crawled under the covers, no longer could she overlook the fact that Brent was the man she longed for. Three years…would they want each other after all that time, or would their relationship dwindle down into friendship and nothing more? Time had a way of changing things. Attachments between two people formed with closeness, not distance.

CHAPTER THIRTEEN

TAYLOR SAT IN her office, contemplating the new Mugful's. She studied the calendar on her desk. She couldn't believe how the time passed. In a week, the newest gourmet beverage shop in Panama would be up and running. Yesterday, she made sure the deliveries were on schedule and performed a last-minute assessment of the facility. Decorated with picturesque tapestries of indigenous appliqués, the interior was a unique blend of old Panama with a bite of Americana thrown in. The purpose was to attract both natives and tourists.

The spot that held the bistro was close to the visitor's center, just a few streets away from the operation. Taylor was glad Mr. Zimmerman had picked that area instead of the local shopping district that typically catered to people who needed to find some place to put up their feet for a few hours, or worse, the airport.

The door opened and her assistant promenaded in, all smiles, carrying Taylor's favorite cappuccino. "Thanks, Brenda. I can use that. My mind is reeling with all the last-minute details. I want to be certain everything is going to be ready for next Tuesday."

"That's good. I can't wait for the opening." Brenda tilted her head as she eyed her boss. "You've been in a much better mood for the past couple weeks. I guess that means you haven't had any more upsetting dreams."

Taylor leaned back and took a sip of the beverage. Letting the rich flavor wash over her tongue, savoring every inch of the taste, she nodded. "It's funny—since Brent and I have started talking over the telephone, those upsetting dreams haven't plagued me anymore. I'm glad...I just don't understand the difference a conversation can make."

A white-colored chair was positioned across from Taylor's workspace. Brenda perched on the soft leather seat. "Well, maybe that's what it's all about. Things don't always happen according to our will. You were fighting any sort of connection you two might have. You were making yourself unhappy. Judging by the way you talk, I believe you and Brent are meant to be, and one day you'll both be at a place in your life to embrace that."

Taylor leaned on her desk with her elbow, propping her chin in her hand. "As much as I like Brent and wish things could be different, our lives are unalike. He's a good man and enjoys working with his hands. To Brent, life is simple. He's the type of guy who just trusts in God and moves on—no matter what. I'm more complicated. I take the world way too seriously—that's the way I am. Even though I believe in God, the biggest pushes in my life are my career and my grandmother."

Silence filled the room. Taylor watched the expression on the woman's face change. Something about the way the lines formed between Brenda's brow and the odd look in her eyes made questioning her important. Taylor scrunched up her nose. "Spit it out, Brenda. What's on your mind?"

"Don't get upset. It's just that I'm at an age where I've learned a few things." Brenda reached up and fiddled with the collar of her blouse, "You know I like you, and you're a great manager. I've watched you these past months, and I've listened to you. I haven't only heard things you have said. I have picked up on a lot of unspoken things. Some, I'm sure even you don't comprehend. Maybe you think all you want is to be Miss Corporate America. But I wonder if there are hopes deep inside that you are afraid to acknowledge. I remember you mentioning that you grew up missing your mom and dad because they traveled a lot. However, here you are, traveling. You spoke about your grandmother keeping you all those years and always being there for you. Perhaps what you assume are needs are just an illusion, because you're afraid of trying for the things that, deep down in your heart, you really want—like a close family, a home. Maybe you're scared that you can't live up to the challenges you might encounter in a steady relationship." Crossing her legs, Brenda continued. "You're the kind of woman who likes to be in command, and the thought of being out of control can be alarming to anyone."

Taylor blinked several times, trying to digest that hard-to-swallow assessment. Part of her was offended, while the other part denied it all. No way. What in the world did Brenda mean about her taking on expectations?

Taylor realized what was essential to her life and how to be happy. What did Brenda know about her anyway? They'd only just become friends.

THAT NIGHT TAYLOR lay in bed, propped on her pillows. She pressed the speed dial. A smile crossed her face at the sound of the older woman's voice on the other end of the telephone. They both exchanged news, and Taylor answered a few questions about her day. "Granny Kay, the grand opening of the new coffee shop is almost here. Then, in a month, I'm planning to fly home for three days. It's already cleared with my boss."

A strange pause stretched out between them.

"That's great. I can't wait to see you. It's been over six months. Will you stay here with Louise and me?"

Taylor wavered a bit with her response. "Well, I do need to go home and collect my mail and pack a few more things. I'll stay the last two days with you and Louise."

Taylor heard a strange gurgle as her grandmother cleared her throat, followed by a second complete silence.

"Granny?"

Then Louise's voice verbalized on the line.

"I'm afraid you have to wait for a minute, Taylor. Kay went to the bathroom."

"What's wrong? Is she all right?"

A loud sigh filled Taylor's ear. "Kay has been sick for a few days, dear. I think it's a virus of some kind. I told her to go to the doctor, but you know your grandmother. She can be stubborn."

"I know. I'll make her promise to go to the doctor. If she promises me something, she will do it."

A weary, miserable-sounding Granny returned to the line. "Taylor, dear, I think I'd better hang up."

After convincing her grandmother to vow to call the doctor for an appointment, she ended the call and placed her cell phone down.

Taylor mulled over the call. In thoughtful meditation, she took hold of her necklace that held the family ring. Closing her eyes,

Taylor found herself bowing her head to talk to God. "Lord, I know I don't speak to you often enough. Please, watch after my grandmother. Keep her safe until I get home. Amen."

There was so much more she wanted to say to Jesus, though she couldn't seem to manage the right words. Why, suddenly, did she get the impression she was being shortchanged here in Panama? There were lots of women who would relish holding a job like hers, working in an exotic, foreign land, all expenses paid. She had it made, hadn't she?

Drawing in a gulp of air, Taylor flipped off the switch to the lamp, and the glow of the light snapped into darkness. Thirty minutes later, she glanced at the clock on her bed stand and caved into her yearning. What was Brent doing? Maybe watching one of those television shows he enjoyed so much. With the minuscule glow from the front of her cell phone, she punched in the now-familiar number, calling the one person whom she wanted to confide in and share about her day and her grandmother.

TUESDAY CAME. MR. ZIMMERMAN flew in for the grand opening. They met at a restaurant for breakfast before the celebration started.

"I stopped by yesterday to greet the staff and check everything out. You did a good job. I'm pleased with what the future holds for this endeavor."

Taylor wiped her mouth on a napkin. Indeed, she was delighted her efforts were well received, and her boss recognized the hard work she had put into the start of the new beverage boutique. For some reason, though, all she could muster up to say was, "Thank you, Mr. Zimmerman."

Scheduled to take place at the same time as a local festival that was happening a couple of streets over, the grand opening had drawn quite a crowd. Everyone clapped as Mr. Zimmerman cut the ribbon to signify the beginning of the new café.

The manager of the store spoke in Spanish and English to all the onlookers. Mr. Zimmerman's face glowed with satisfaction. He leaned toward Taylor as he listened to the speech and whispered, "You know the word Panama is supposed to mean an abundance of fish? Well…the name Mugful's represents an abundance of coffee." He laughed at his own humor.

With the beginning of the new Mugful's underway, they walked through the boulevard, checking out the art and woodwork. In the distance, Reggae music played. After they enjoyed lunch, Mr. Zimmerman sat in Taylor's office, scanning the files to ensure everything was to his specifications and all the loose ends for opening a new business sufficiently tied.

As the day wore on, Taylor relinquished her office, temporarily moving her laptop into the vacant space that housed a desk and chair, giving her boss the biggest room to work in. She spent the rest of the day coordinating details for advertisements and coupons to draw attention to Mugful's in Panama.

"GOOD MORNING, TAYLOR. Are you glad the open is over?"

Taylor snagged a cup and poured her drink. "Yes. I spoke with Mr. Zimmerman earlier, before he departed for North Carolina. He seemed pleased with the way it all turned out."

The assistant shuffled papers on her desk. "That Mr. Zimmerman sure is a no-nonsense person."

Taylor turned to go into her office. "He does have a one-track mind. He's determined that this company will move to the top."

If Taylor thought yesterday was fast-paced, the events of today threw her into a whirling spin. She worked almost nonstop, dealing with last-minute problems because of new employees and a manager who was great with customers, but a little green in the supervisory area. Nevertheless, Taylor believed once the man took hold of the position, he would be dedicated to the company for years.

Brenda had to leave an hour before closing, and Taylor locked up the office for the night. As she walked across the street, she made a fast stop at the nearest deli. All she had on her mind was a hot bath and sitting outside in the lounger with a sandwich.

A SONG PLAYED in the quiet of Taylor's bedroom, rousing her. She peered at her clock. At first, she'd feared the noise was her alarm and morning had come too soon. When the time told her that wasn't the case, she convinced herself the music coming from somewhere in the building.

Had she been dreaming? No, she didn't believe so.

Thank goodness, the weird nightmares seemed to have disappeared for now. The last one happened weeks ago. To this day, she wasn't sure of all the things she'd blurted out over the telephone, but she could just imagine. Brent could really get to her. She still couldn't understand why she'd admitted to him that he was the only guy she wanted to be around, even if all they did was talk.

Now awake, whether she wanted to be or not, she twisted at the chain around her neck and scrunched her face at the memory. Such comments should be left unsaid—instead, she also had to blurt out that she hoped he was available when she came home.

Groaning, she threw aside the covers and rose out of bed. All of this was unlike her. Never had she said things without thinking about them first—let alone talked in her sleep. Oh, well, it was done now. As her mom used to say—no need to cry over spilled milk. Nothing could take those words away, and besides, Taylor couldn't deny, deep inside, they were true.

After getting a drink of water, she returned to bed. Just as she dozed back to sleep, her mobile phone rang out another jingle. This time, she recognized the sound. She grabbed her cell from the nightstand and answered.

Louise's unsteady voice rang out. "Taylor, something has happened to Kay."

CHAPTER FOURTEEN

"LOUISE, WHAT'S WRONG?" Taylor's heart skipped several beats as she scrambled to the side of the bed. "Is she okay? What happened?"

"She was just so sick. I took her to the emergency room this evening, and they checked her into a room. She doesn't have much strength. She's dehydrated, and the physician said it was because of being nauseated. They're trying to find out why she's having stomach pains and vomiting so much. For now, they're giving her a saline IV and have scheduled tests for the morning. They think it may just be gastroenteritis. I hope it's nothing more, but she's been sick a good while."

Taylor gnawed on her bottom lip as she listened to the news. "I was planning to take a flight to North Carolina in a few weeks. I'll try to make arrangements to come earlier."

Clearing her throat, Louise replied, "Why don't you wait a few hours on that? See what the doctor says about the tests before you come all that way. I'll call you as soon as I know more."

Taylor tossed her cell phone on the bed and stood. Pushing her hair from her face, she walked the perimeter of the room. The flu...perfectly normal. People catch the virus all the time.

Taylor looked at the big number four glaring on the clock. *I can't go back to sleep.*

Grabbing her clothes, she headed to the shower. "I'll wait and see, but if she needs me, nothing will stand in my way."

"GOOD MORNING...TAYLOR? What's wrong?"

Taylor attempted a sedate smile. "I received a call early this morning from Louise, my grandmother's friend. Granny Kay is in the hospital with an infection or something. It doesn't appear to be serious, not that we know of, but I'm a bit upset. She's not as young as she used to be."

"Oh, Taylor, I'm sorry. I'll pray for her. What sort of infection does she have?"

"Some kind of stomach problem. She's throwing up a lot and very weak. Thanks for the prayers, Brenda. I know they will mean a lot to Granny Kay."

Taylor worked through the slow day, overwhelmed with problems. Her grandmother's condition played on her mind nonstop. Granny Kay was never one to get sick. The occasional cold, sure, and she took medicine for high cholesterol. Other than that, her health wasn't usually an issue. Though the fall she had taken months ago slowed her down, by the time Taylor came to Panama, her grandmother was back to her old self again.

The memory of a dream she had involving her grandmother and her dad dashed into her mind. She couldn't figure out what the image meant, and it bothered her a lot. *If I don't hear something by four this afternoon, I'm calling the hospital.*

TAYLOR CURLED ON her sofa in her nightgown, anything but relaxed. She'd spoken with Granny Kay fifteen minutes earlier. The older woman sounded cheery enough. Taylor suspected that was a put-on. Granny Kay was generous to a fault with Taylor—if she didn't want Taylor to worry, she would downplay her sickness.

Taylor's heart longed to be in North Carolina. To be sitting beside her grandmother's bed, holding her hand—just as she'd done months ago when Granny Kay had taken that fall.

Being so far from her didn't sit right.

THE NEXT EVENING, Taylor spoke to Louise. "I wanted to talk to you before I called Granny Kay's room. How's she doing? What do the doctors say?"

"Kay's stomach condition isn't improving. She continued to heave today, and a fever has set in. The doctor is concerned. With the way her stomach is staying upset, they can't pump fluids in her fast enough to keep her from becoming more dehydrated." Louise paused. "She's so weak, she can't even hold her head up."

Taylor called the hospital and attempted to talk to her grandmother, though she couldn't understand much of what Kay said. Louise returned to the room and once again took the phone when Kay became sick. Kay's lifelong friend promised to let Taylor know when the additional test results came back.

Glancing at her watch, Taylor considered her supervisor's routine. The man should be in his office at this time of day. She dialed his number and mentally rehearsed the conversation she'd planned the night before if her grandmother wasn't improving. She'd had enough. Even though her schedule had her returning home for a visit in less than three weeks, she needed to leave now. If something were to happen to her grandmother and she was thousands of miles away, she would never be able to live with herself.

After the usual greeting, she listened with all the patience she could muster while her boss reviewed a few ideas for the new beverage store. Taylor tried to pay attention to the comments about the expansion. Even though she was pleased that he approved of the operations here in Panama, Taylor's mind lingered on her plans. Scheduling a flight. What to pack. Whether to ask Brent or Louise to pick her up at the airport, or to rent a car. She bided her time, waiting to speak. As much as her career meant, only thing was on her mind at the moment—being at Granny's side.

"Mr. Zimmerman, a situation has come up with my grandmother. She has been hospitalized. They can't manage to find out what is wrong, and she's getting weaker each day. Because of her age, it has me concerned. I know you okayed my travel to North Carolina for a later date, but I need to leave in the next day or so."

A void filled the line, followed by a discreet cough. "I realize you have family obligations. You also are aware a lot can happen in two and a half weeks. We need someone in Panama to counteract negative issues that might pop up." He declared his concerns as if he were talking to a child. "The first few months of any new business are always the most important. Perhaps you can keep close tabs with her over the phone. After all, the time will pass soon enough."

Taylor ended the call, slamming the phone down on the couch cushion. Feeling as if steam puffed out of her ears, her face blaring hot, she almost leaped out of her seat.

She paced the room and fumed as she recalled the unpaid overtime she'd put in and vacation hours gone unused, all because of her dedication to the company.

Then she stopped in front of the window and rubbed her arms. Why had she believed that if she ever did need to take care of personal matters, her needs would be regarded with respect?

AS SENSELESS AS it seemed to lie down, Taylor positioned herself in bed. Even though she feared sleep wouldn't come anytime soon, rest was necessary. Flat on her back, she struggled with the conversation with Mr. Zimmerman. Her worries wavered between the corporate owner of Mugful's, her grandmother, and finally Brent.

Just as Taylor was about to reach for her cell and punch in his number, the familiar beach theme played, signaling a call.

She snuggled her head in the pillow, comforted to hear his masculine voice. "I'm sorry to hear about Kay being in the hospital. I hope everything's going to be all right."

Still harboring anxiety from her conversation with Mr. Zimmerman, Taylor welcomed the opportunity to unload her stress. "I'm *infuriated* with my boss. The man is close-minded. Nothing matters except the company. He wouldn't even consider my flying home earlier than planned." Taylor sat and switched on the small bedside light. "I was coming to Liberty Cove in a couple weeks anyway. Honestly, I'm thinking about leaving before then, no matter what he says. I'm waiting for your aunt to call. She said the doctors were running more tests. They can't find out why Granny's so nauseated and continues to run a fever. I don't feel good about this whole situation. I need to be there."

"I will keep her in my prayers. We have to trust in God and believe that Kay will be fine. Nevertheless, your boss sounds like an ogre. Don't let him bully you."

"He won't. He has another think coming if thinks I'll choose Mugful's over Granny."

"Atta girl. I don't mean to change the subject, but when you do fly home and see Kay, maybe we can carve out a couple of hours to spend together."

"I would like to see you. But my visit won't change the facts. I will have to return to Panama, and I'll be here for a while. Where does that leave us?"

"I realize you made a commitment to the beverage shop in Central America. I stand by what I said months ago. We can take one day at a time and see how things go. I found out a long time ago it's best to wait on the Lord. Sometimes God takes a while to lead us where we should be. In the meantime, I'll take any chance I get to be with you."

BEFORE PLACING HER cell on the edge of the table, Taylor checked the volume. In case she fell asleep, she wanted to be sure to hear it ringing.

Momentarily, thanks to Brent, her mind was off Mr. Zimmerman and her grandmother. The prospect of seeing him was thrilling but also brought on anxiety. Talking on the phone was one thing. But seeing him...being in his arms again—could she handle it?

Could he?

She didn't want to string Brent along. She had to be away from him for almost three years. Was it fair?

THE NEXT DAY proved busy. Taylor had Brenda oversee a few issues, stating with a mix-up in supplies. She spent most of an hour talking to the distributor and confirming delivery schedules. After lunch, a call from the manager of the new café had her rushing out the door. Small problems and necessary changes continued to occupy the day for the newest Mugful's.

That evening, relief flooded Taylor as she walked inside her luxury condo. At work she was swamped, but her grandmother plagued her mind. Even with a hectic schedule, the time ticked away while she waited for her cell phone to ring and update her on her grandmother's medical tests.

Taylor microwaved a frozen dinner while deciding to dial the number to the hospital and speak to the doctor. The buzzer sounded, signifying her food was finished. Grabbing a kitchen towel, Taylor placed the container on the granite bar, along with her silverware, and went to fetch her phone from her purse. Just as she was about to punch in a number on her mobile, a din blared, indicating an incoming call.

"Taylor, its Brent. Louise wanted me to call you. They're rushing Kay to the operating room. The doctor discovered her problem was appendicitis. Her appendix ruptured. No one knows yet how bad it is."

"No..." Taylor's heart seemed to stop. She pressed her fingers to her eyelids. Her mind spun with the hard facts. She was thousands of miles away. She couldn't just hop in her car and hit the highway. "I don't know what to do. Brent, what happens now?"

An awkward moment of silence stretched before he spoke. "I don't know. The doctor said something about infection and possible complications."

Taylor's hand shook as she put her fingers to her mouth. As if someone punched her in the gut, her stomach clenched. In an almost inaudible voice, she said, "Brent, I need to hang up now."

Her habit of pacing had her strolling around the room. Fears and anger raced through her mind as she reached for her neck, sliding the heirloom ring back and forth on its chain. Regardless of the new store's needs, she wanted to be in North Carolina. She had to believe her dedication to Mugful's was worth something in an emergency. Without further plans, she dialed Mr. Zimmerman's cell number.

The rings stretched on. He wasn't answering his phone. All she could do was leave a message, with an explanation of her intention to catch the first available flight to the States.

Taylor rushed around, tossing things in her suitcase. She didn't know how she'd manage, but she intended to be on a flight heading home as soon as possible. Picking up her cell, she dialed Brenda.

"Taylor, what's wrong?"

"My grandmother has been rushed to the operating room. Her appendix burst. I'm going home. I just wanted to let you know. If anything needs attention, you can handle matters. We've already discussed the basics for when I was scheduled to leave in a few weeks. Follow those instructions." Taylor lowered her voice in a defeated tone. "I...I don't know how this is going to play out...all I know is that I have to go home. I'll call you when I can."

Next, Taylor punched in the digits for the airport, waiting for someone who worked in the reservations department to pick up the receiver. After being put on hold for what seemed like eternity, a male voice came back on the line. His English was seeped in a

Spanish accent. Taylor had learned some of the language, although by no means was she fluent. Thankfully, his dialogue was blended enough that she understood.

As Taylor ended the call, she was satisfied. Luck was on her side. A recent cancellation made scheduling an urgent flight possible. Even though the ticket cost her ten percent more, she was glad to have a seat on the plane. Barring any problems, she would be on her way to the United States shortly.

TAYLOR SEATED HERSELF in one of the chairs in the airport and tried to get comfortable. Every five minutes she caught herself looking at the big clock on the wall, watching the hands move until it was time to board. Her cell phone rang.

"Louise, how is Granny Kay?"

"She's still in the operating room. One of the nurses said something about infection. She called it peritonitis. I don't mind telling you, I'm worried. I called your parents."

Taylor eyed the digital screen on the wall. Shortly, she would be in the air. Getting up out of the plastic chair, she lifted her bag and made her way toward the boarding line.

"I'm on my way home. I should be there around midnight." Taylor closed her eyes and pinched the bridge of her noise with her free hand. Louise offered to pray.

In silence, Taylor soaked in the words the older lady said to God. At the end of the plea, she added her own tidings that expressed her adoration for the woman who had taught her about love. For the first time, Taylor realized her grandmother had also taught her about their merciful God. Kay's everyday life demonstrated the grace the Lord presented to His children.

JUST AS SHE entering the line and walking the last few feet that would lead her home, Taylor's favorite song boomed out into the crowd. Glancing at the number, dread closed in. As she put the cell phone to her ear, emotions she couldn't name squeezed her throat. As if hands were around her neck, the muscles tightened. In a thick, dry voice, she answered.

"Taylor, what are you doing?" Mr. Zimmerman's agitated tone exploded into her ear. "I told you the coming weeks were important to this company. We discussed the trip and decided you would wait. I believed you were the person I could count on to make this venture a success. Now, I wonder."

Taylor put her weight heavier on one leg and tapped the toe of the other foot as the words he shouted stung her ear. His I-only-care-about-my-company attitude shrieked from his vocal chords. His response rustled her pride, and regardless, she had made up her mind.

No matter the outcome, Taylor had to do this. Her grandmother was always there for her, and now it was her turn to repay the dedication she had received while growing up.

Taylor gritted her teeth. "Mr. Zimmerman, I hear what you're saying. However, I have total faith in Brenda Stone and the manager of the new café. This is something I have to do. After all the hard work I have put into Mugful's, you should know the company means a great deal to me. But my grandmother's life comes first."

With that, she exhaled a loud breath and hit the end button, stopping any chance he had of issuing some impossible decree.

As she moved up in the line, she noticed a few people gawking her way. No doubt, she had spoken a bit loudly. She didn't care. She kept her chin up and searched for seat 7-B.

TAYLOR BUSIED HERSELF with a book. Later, she played a game on her phone. Tossing her head back, she stared at the interior of the plane. With curiosity, she watched a man whisper to a lady sitting beside him. The woman returned the whisper with a shy grin. A few seats below the couple, a heavy-set woman checked the lock on child's seat belt.

As Taylor took in the people around her, the harsh conversation she'd had with her manager flashed through her mind, causing her to relive the things she'd said. She contemplated ways to smooth things over. Other than her grandmother, her career was the most important thing.

How could her boss not understand the gravity of the situation? Her grandmother was having surgery!

Straightening her top, she brushed at an invisible piece of lint. She couldn't think about Mr. Zimmerman right now, not with something more significant going on.

Taylor rested her head against the plane's vinyl seat and pondered the days spent with her favorite member of the family. Then her thoughts traveled to her mom and dad. She did love them, even if her feelings for them were different. Taylor never questioned their love—of course, they were more distant than her grandparents, but she understood both cared about her. Perhaps she distorted things, believing her parents chose to put other needs before her.

Her dad's parents were totally opposite. For as long as she could remember, her grandmother had always showered her with love.

Taylor's mind traveled to the days before they lost her grandfather. They had a ritual all of their own. Every Sunday before the night worship service, the two of them would go out for ice cream. Those special moments and the heart-to-heart talks over chocolate-chip mint…how she missed them. Her grandfather's death had been hard on Taylor.

How had her grandmother coped? There was no question—Granny Kay missed her husband very much. Over the years, Taylor had witnessed a love between both that was unshakeable. What had surprised Taylor was the continued faith her grandmother clung to, long after her husband's death.

Taylor couldn't remember a single time her grandmother showed bitterness over losing her mate. It was as if she understood and accepted the way things were, always clinging to God to lead her past the hurt.

As she twisted her head toward the porthole in the plane, desperation threatened, trying to take over her emotions. An unhappy ending for her grandmother flaunted itself, dangling in the air, taunting her.

Taylor's old habit had her grabbing the sapphire stone that hung against her skin. She closed her eyes and uttered a hushed prayer. Once again, she appealed to Jesus, but this time from deep within her soul.

She yanked her hand away from her neck. Silly, of course, but she thought she felt heat from the gem penetrating her fingers.

THE FIRST THING Taylor did when she landed was call Louise, though it went to voicemail. She was glad that the older ladies at least saw the need to purchase cell phones after her grandmother's fall.

She had taken a cab to her condominium, though she never went inside, only tossed her belongings into her compact sports car. Now she headed to Liberty Cove Memorial Hospital. The facility wasn't big, like Duke Medical Center in Raleigh, yet it had top-notch doctors.

She tried Louise again, and this time her aunt's friend answered.

"Louise, how is Granny Kay?" Taylor waited, anxious for an answer. After several seconds of silence, she asked the question again. "Tell me she made it through the surgery."

"She's in intensive care. Dr. Barnes said her appendix had developed a hole, which caused a leakage. They cleaned her abdominal cavity. All we can do for now is to hope the intravenous antibiotics they're giving her start working."

TAYLOR SAT IN the waiting room, thankful that the nurse had allowed her to see her grandmother for a few minutes. Granny Kay was sleeping now. The medical staff seemed optimistic that Kay was going to be okay. They credited her improvement, though slight as it was, to the drugs that seemed to be fighting off the infection. At least her grandmother no longer had a fever. That was a good sign.

Taylor bowed her head. She gave the credit to the Lord. *Yes, God, You made doctors smart. You are The Almighty, the One who makes miracles possible.*

AS THE HOURS whittled away at the hospital, Taylor and Louise shared casual conversation. At some point, Taylor managed to convince the older woman to go home and rest.

Now, she sat in the padded wooden chair with her legs drawn underneath her, watching the clock. Taylor sipped on a poor excuse for a cappuccino from the hospital vending machine. Out of the corner of her eye, she caught sight of that well-known crooked smile and leapt to her feet.

Brent swooped in, and without one bit of hesitation, embraced her and planted a kiss upon her lips. "Taylor, I'm so glad to see you. I'm not happy that it has to be like this."

She soaked in the warmth from his body and the security his presence offered. "Yeah, I know. My grandmother is sleeping now. Her temperature has dropped, at least. I'm just worried she's sleeping way too much. I'm not even sure she knows I'm here."

Taylor sat back down and Brent took the chair beside her. Her heart leapt when he reached out and took hold of her fingers, enclosing them in his strong hand. Never, in all her life, would she have believed that a man with calluses would be the object of her desire. Yes, Brent was different. He donned a suit on Sunday mornings, and that was it. The man had a degree in architecture and could be in an office, designing impressive buildings, yet he would rather do manual labor. He enjoyed swinging a hammer more than drawing blueprints.

Smiling, she looked into his eyes. If she let down her resolve, the intensity of his ocean-blues would burn into her. His brow wrinkled, laden with concern, and she caught a glimpse of something else—a compassion that wanted to claim her soul. To melt away any doubts she had about life or the two of them.

For the next several hours, he sat beside her faithfully. They talked about Panama and the construction projects Brent had finished. Taylor squirmed in her seat when he made small references about the future—their future—feeling as if she were on a carnival ride. Her mind whirled back and forth. As troubled as she was about her grandmother's illness, she also fretted at the implications of things to come. Would she be fired for leaving?

Never receive her chance at becoming Vice President of Operations in the corporate firm of Mugful's?

If she committed to Brent, where would her life end up? As a stay-at-home mom in jogging pants, with spit-up in her hair? Would she cease wearing makeup and spend her days in frumpy elastic pants, waking up one day to realize the years had passed her by?

Would her whole life go down the drain, yielded to her desire for Brent?

When she thought of the alternative, returning to Panama and trying to appease Mr. Zimmerman…leaving Granny…she was ready to chuck her expensive pumps out the window.

Taylor tried hard to stop her mind from conjuring up images, scenes of an everyday life with this man.

The doctor entered the little room, and Taylor exhaled in relief. Now she could get some answers about her grandmother.

"Dr. Barnes, how is Granny Kay doing?

The short graying man gave Taylor a sympathetic smile. "She's doing as well as we can expect. Because of her age, it was hard to detect the appendicitis. It's good we got to her when we did. Any later… I did have to clean the abdominal cavity of infectious organisms. Ms. Harrison, don't be surprised if your grandmother sleeps a lot in the next couple days. We have her on some strong medication. The good news is she's responding. Her body just needs time to heal. Appendicitis is hard on anybody, and much more difficult for an older person. Now we'll monitor her and continue the intravenous medication. It may take a week or so, but I expect a full recovery. Perhaps tomorrow we will move her to a private room."

After the doctor left, Brent escorted Taylor to the cafeteria and insisted she eat. Later, he received a call about a job and had to leave.

Now alone, Taylor paced the room. Her hand fiddled with the chain around her neck. Her thoughts centered on the past hours. In an almost inaudible voice, she mumbled the words, "Thank you, Lord."

EARLY THE NEXT morning, Louise Matthews walked in. "Taylor, how's Kay?"

A wide smile stretched across Taylor's face. "She's doing much better. They're going to move her to a room this afternoon. We can then see her anytime we want instead of a few minutes four times a day. Everything's going to be all right."

After chatting to her grandmother's best friend for another half-hour, Taylor left to manage a few hours rest away from the hospital.

On her way to the car, her mobile phone announced a call. She looked on the front at her father's number flashing.

"What's going on with Mom? How did the surgery go?"

"Granny Kay is in intensive care now. The plans are to move her to a room later today. Doctor Barnes says she'll need lots of IVs. They're confident Granny Kay is going to be all right. Where are you?"

Why aren't you here?

"I can't believe I couldn't get there earlier. I should have been at the hospital." Her father's refined voice traveled smoothly. He didn't have the expected southern drawl but rather more of a mixed accent, since he traveled across many states most of his life. "Your mom and I have had a bit of a time getting out of Alaska. We'll be there in a little while. You tell your grandmother we love her."

TAYLOR PULLED ONTO the tree-lined road that led to Louise's stucco and brick home, where she'd be staying since it was closer to the hospital. She couldn't help gazing at the pine trees in a different light. The country roads of Liberty Cove may not be a match for Central America, but to her the area was a head above the rest. Rural North Carolina with its springy pines trees was where her heart lay. *I see now...I love being close to home.*

Taylor used the key Louise had provided and let herself in. In no time, she was fast asleep in the guest bedroom.

TAYLOR YAWNED AS she stretched her arms over her head and peered at the picture perched on a dresser—a picture of Jesus knocking on a wooden door.

As soon as she showered and left for the hospital, she would be able to see Granny Kay in her private room. With that thought, she leapt out of bed. An abrupt noise from her phone made her turn. She had put her cell phone on vibrate in the hospital, and now it buzzed, scraping against wood and beckoning her to answer.

Drawing a hard wind, she answered the phone, not ready for what waited on the other side. "I have been trying to reach you for hours."

"I'm sorry, Mr. Zimmerman. I must have been asleep."

To his credit, Mr. Zimmerman asked about her grandmother. Although he was just being cordial, she answered, "Granny Kay had a bad time. Her appendix burst, and infection started to set in before they found out what was wrong. If they hadn't discovered what was causing the pain, she could have died. The doctor said it will be two weeks or more before she gets back on her feet."

"Well, it's good that she will be all right." Mr. Zimmerman continued speaking in a non-emotional, rushed dialogue. "If you plan to be in Liberty Cove for a couple weeks, I'm going to send Avery Thomas to Panama City to oversee Mugful's. It's imperative that someone be there to handle any problems. You know how situations arise with a new business, and as I stated before, the first month is critical to the branch's success.

"A make it or break it status quo, they say. From the very beginning, Avery has expressed a desire to lead this project. He can make the necessary commitment." Then in a chastening voice, he added, "I want you to come to the office by the end of next week. We will talk about your position with the company."

Taylor felt as if a boulder flattened her like putty. Too shocked to try and comprehend what he meant, she responded in a flat tone. "I understand. I'll come in Friday after lunch."

TAYLOR STEPPED INSIDE the small corner room where her grandmother lay sleeping. The older woman's face appeared ghost white, almost as pale as the sheet pulled up to her chin.

As Taylor walked over to the bed, her heart sank at the sight of the once-vibrant lady who now appeared frail and twenty pounds lighter.

She didn't need to lose any weight. Shaking her head, Taylor reached out and touched the snow-white hair that lay in a bob—the same style her grandmother had worn for the past ten years.

Was this her fault? Had her leaving broken Granny Kay's heart and led her down the path to poor health?

Kay Harrison moved her head to the side in slow motion and smiled. A beam of joy showed in her eyes and radiated a smile to her lips.

"Taylor…it's good to see you, dear. How long are you going to be here?"

Taylor rubbed her grandmother wavy locks as she considered the question. "I'm here now Granny Kay. That's what matters."

The older woman clutched Taylor's hand, her voice gaining more strength. "I'm glad. Maybe we can talk later." Her gaze moved to the ring hanging from a chain around Taylor's neck. "I love seeing that ring dangling at your collar." Forging a little burst of added strength, she grinned. "When I feel more like talking, remind me to tell you about the special stone you're wearing."

A lab technician entered the room with empty vials and walked to the other side of the bed, preparing to take blood. On impulse, Taylor touched the glimmering stone while she hushed her grandmother. "Be a good patient. I'm going to step out and buy a cola. I'll be back in a few minutes."

Taylor made her way to the waiting room and was sliding a dollar bill into the vending machine when Brent's sister, Daisy, approached. "How is Kay?"

Taylor turned and smiled at the familiar woman with her turquoise jewelry—a friendly sight. "She's weak, but she'll be fine. I thought you were moving with your husband to Nags Head."

They walked toward the section of chairs as Daisy replied. "I am. My husband wanted to help the other veterinarian become accustomed to the office and the patients. We plan on leaving in a month. Plus, I still haven't sold the boutique, and it will affect the asking price if I close the business. I may need to hire a temporary manager. I've tried selling it myself, but it's time to bring a realtor on board, I suppose."

Daisy's expression grew inquisitive as she noticed the chain hanging from Taylor's neck. "My, that's a beautiful ring. It's unique and sparkles a lot for such a dark color." Laughing, she displayed her adorned hands, adding, "You know I love jewelry."

"My grandmother gave it to me."

Daisy admired the ring once more then continued talking. "Before I forget, I want ask you a question. What's the name of the realtor who is handling the sale of your grandmother's home? I may call and ask them to sell my store."

Taylor pressed her finger to her lips then responded. "Hmmm, I don't remember. I'll find her business card and let you know."

Daisy stood, nodding in the direction of the exit. "I'm going to visit with Kay a minute, then I have to get back to the shop."

"Tell her I'll see her in a few minutes."

THE REST OF the day, Taylor hung out in the room with her grandmother. She ate a takeout lunch while Granny Kay spooned in chicken broth. They made idle chit-chat, and Taylor tried to keep the conversations short so as not to wear on her grandmother's health. Kay was improving, but she had a ways to go and would be on a liquid diet for a few more days.

After Granny Kay had dinner, Taylor kissed the side of her grandmother's face, saying goodbye for the night. "I'll be late arriving tomorrow, Granny Kay. I promised to swing by and give Daisy the number of the realtor you're using. She needs to place her dress shop in the hands of someone who can help her sell. She's eager to move into the retirement home in Nags Head."

Her grandmother shifted her head on the pillow. Her words came out slower than usual. "Yes, I remember her telling Louise and me about it. I think…the telephone number is in the desk drawer in the hall."

Taylor caught the odd expression in her grandmother's eyes. "Are you okay?"

"Will you go by our family home and check on things?"

Taylor repositioned her hair clip. "Okay, but doesn't the realtor do that?"

Granny Kay looked away. "I haven't signed a contract with her yet to sell the estate."

Openmouthed, Taylor stared at her grandmother, taken aback by the length of time that had passed. She bit her tongue.

After all, her grandmother had been ill for a while and was getting older.

TAYLOR WOKE EARLY. It dawned on her that she hadn't had any bad dreams since being back in North Carolina. She hoped that was over. Because Granny Kay was getting stronger, the upcoming business meeting with Mr. Zimmerman lay heavy on her mind. *God, what will I do if I lose my job? How do I start over?* She grabbed the phone and punched out the long number for Brenda Stone in Panama. "Taylor, hi! It's good to hear your voice. How's your grandmother?"

"Doing much better. They had to do an appendectomy, but thank God, she will be all right. What's going on at the office?"

She waited as she listened to shuffling sounds. "It's a smidgeon different around here. Mr. Thomas is a fine man, but I miss you being in command."

Brenda filled her in on the highlights of the Panama City shop. Before Taylor ended the call, Brenda said, "When are you coming back?"

Stalling before she responded, she realized she couldn't answer that question. "I can't say that I will return. I have a meeting with Mr. Zimmerman. He wasn't too happy about me coming home early. Truth be told, he was furious."

A heavy sigh sounded on the end of the line. "I know. He called the next day, booming into the receiver, and informed me he was sending another manager. I like you and wish you were running things. Sometimes, though, situations happen for a reason. Don't beat yourself up about anything. Your grandmother will be fine—that's what's important. You have my home number. Call me."

PULLING INTO THE curved drive to the family estate had Taylor's pulse racing. Why was she so excited to see this house again?

She opened the front door, entering into the now-open-concept living and dining area. The hardwood floors gleamed with warm tones. She walked into the kitchen and then peeped into the guest room that had been her domain for a short while. The bed sat in the middle of the floor, sporting the comforter she'd washed and placed there before leaving.

Taylor moved toward the main living area. At a slower pace, she took another look at the vast, empty space. A feeling of tranquility swept through her as she drifted around from one room to another and soaked in the view. Staring out of the library window, she fiddled with the gem hanging from her neck. Out of the blue, she spoke into the air. "Yes, I'm home." She jerked around as if she expected someone to overhear her words. Where in the world did that come from? *Why did I say such a thing?*

TAYLOR PULLED INTO the parking lot of the strip mall that housed Daisy's Boutique and walked into the store. "I brought you the name of that realtor. I believe while I'm here I'll check out that new outfit you have hanging in the window."

Daisy smiled and walked with Taylor to the rack where the two-piece outfits and casual pants hung. Taylor couldn't resist selecting a few items while she listened to Daisy talk about the store. After trying on a gray striped pantsuit, she paid for her purchases and left, heading back to the hospital.

A smile crossed her face as she approached her grandmother's room and heard family laughter drifting into the hallway. She hushed her steps and stood at the entrance.

Her mother and father sat in chairs across from her grandmother, engrossed in fun banter. She observed her parents. Taylor's mom was a fashion diva. Today, she wore a turquoise pantsuit. Her straight hair was styled in a trendy haircut and colored to hide her true age. Even the few extra pounds her mother appeared to have added since she last saw her didn't take away from the woman's charm. She had to give the lady credit. Sara Harrison dressed in style.

She eyed her father again. He wore a pair of the khakis he loved so well and a navy blazer. The man's thick mass of curls had thinned a bit and was grayer. One of the downfalls of her grandmother's family—as far as Taylor was concerned—was the natural curly hair.

Her father spotted her first and hurried out of the chair. "Taylor, honey, it's good to see my girl."

Both her parents rushed to hug their daughter.

"When did you get in?"

"Late last night. We didn't want to wake you, knowing we would see you today. We even had breakfast with Mom this morning. We plan on spending the entire day with her." Dad chuckled. "That is, if the nurses don't run us out. Taylor, if you have the time, I thought we could go out to a late dinner together." With a wink, he added, "You can fill me in on everything that's been going on."

AFTER A DAY spent together in Granny Kay's room, Taylor and her parents drove to a nearby restaurant. The first topic of conversation revolved around the renovations. Taylor then answered all their concerns about Granny Kay's health. Taylor's dad waited patiently for his wife and daughter to finish their girl talk. When the waiter came and refilled the drinks, he asked if she planned to return to Panama.

"Things don't look good, Dad. When I left early, Mr. Zimmerman wasn't pleased. He sent a replacement to Central America. I'm supposed to have a meeting with him Friday. I'll know more about my future then." Taylor placed her glass on the white tablecloth, focusing her attention on her parents. "Dad, Panama's beautiful. My home is here, though. I honestly don't know how you two travel the way you do. If my job required me to move about a lot, I think I would grow exasperated."

Taylor's mom patted her daughter's hand. "Dear, it's good that you enjoy being in one place. Your dad and I have always like seeing the world. We discovered a long time ago that life is just too short not to enjoy every minute of it doing what makes you content. Remember, Taylor, life is about making the best of each day and striving to be happy at whatever you do. "

AFTER ANOTHER LONG day at the hospital with her grandmother and parents, Taylor sat beside Brent at the pizzeria. They talked about her parents, who'd recently shared news of a project they were heading up in Alaska, and every so often Brent hinted at the possibility of them having a future one day. After the meal, they sat close in the vinyl-covered booth and nursed a pitcher of tea. Brent held her hand, massaging her fingers.

These frequent dinners with him since she'd arrived home were becoming addicting.

"What happens now? When Kay comes home from the hospital…will you return to Panama?"

Taylor swallowed hard. A twinge of something she couldn't identify tried to surface. Her mind had been spinning since the start of their date, riddled with unspoken thoughts, while Brent worked in suggestions of them being together. She considered the words her mom had spoken in relation to being happy in life. But Taylor had yet to figure out what would make her joy complete.

Last year, her satisfactions lay in her job at Mugful's, with her eyes set on climbing the ladder of success. That was before she met Brent, prior to the scare with her grandmother. The entire scene in the intensive care unit forced her to face the fact that her grandmother wasn't invincible. One day, she would die. Before now, Taylor had never let her mind wander to a place and time where the woman she loved so much wouldn't be in her life. Now, for some reason, work wasn't the most important aspect, and she couldn't help dwelling on things that lay ahead. What would her daily existence be like without her family?

Taylor touched the sapphire ring around her neck. The events over the past week had brought her to her knees. Her life had hit the skids. It was as if God slapped her in the face with a dose of reality. A lesson on what was significant.

Snapping out of the familiar track her mind pulled her in the past couple days, she smiled at Brent. But the words she wanted to say stuck in her throat. No, until she talked to her boss, she shouldn't lead him on. There was a small chance he would insist she return to Panama. Until she made solid decisions, she didn't have anything to offer.

"I have a meeting with Mr. Zimmerman the end of the week. I'll know then what the future holds."

THAT NIGHT THE two of them stood on Louise's front porch. Brent toyed with the curls in Taylor's hair. With a charm as thick as gravy, he dropped little remarks about her beauty and the attraction he held in his heart for her. Planting short, light kisses on her cheek, he moved his mouth to her neck. Lifting his head, he looked into her eyes. Brent's voice came out husky, laced with emotion. "Taylor, I need you to be part of my life. I've never felt this way about any woman before."

Taylor's heart fluttered and told her what she wanted. She clasped her lips tight and dared not mention it. This past week had indeed changed her outlook on life, and the changes scared her.

Their goodnight kiss was deep and searching, asking all the questions Taylor needed the answers to.

A FEW DAYS later, as Taylor drove her parents to the airport for their flight back to Alaska, Louise stayed with Kay, catching up on the gossip.

"Kay, you gave me a scare. I don't think I have been down on my knees to the Lord in whole year as much as I was the first three days you were admitted to the hospital."

A look of serenity shone on Kay's face as she stared out the open window, listening to a bird chirp in the nearby courtyard. "I must admit I was a bit fearful myself. Then, when the doctor moved me to this room, I realized something." Turning to face her friend, she continued. "You know the Bible section in Romans? The one that says things will work together for the people who love the Lord? That verse popped in my head. It was then I discerned God had a plan all of His own. The Lord may not have brought Taylor back to me the way I thought He would. She is here, though, and I'm going to be fine. Jesus is so wonderful. I feel in my heart that Taylor will end up staying home and finding the true meaning of her life—one that doesn't revolve around a desk in an office."

"Let's hope it includes my dear nephew. That boy is crazy about her."

Louise left an hour later and promised to see her friend the next day.

THE ELEVATOR DOOR opened. Taylor stepped into the hall and approached the hospital room. Granny Kay was sitting up, leaning against a pillow. The older woman's color had returned, and the doctor had suggested possibly letting her go home sometime in the coming week. Taylor walked into the room and stood close to the bed

"I hated to see your dad and mom leave. But...I realized long ago that traveling is what keeps them young. I suppose if they had to stop gallivanting around the country, it would take a toll on their happiness. You've always been my joy, like a daughter instead of a grandchild."

"I love you very much, Granny."

"The good thing about their travels was that I had the privilege of spending a lot of time with you. I could never regret the time we had together." With a deep sigh, she gazed at Taylor's neck. The jewelry flickered in the light that shone overhead. A childlike grin showed on her wrinkled face. Her eyes gleamed.

"What is it?"

Motioning in the direction of the closest seat, Granny Kay indicated to Taylor to take a seat. "Now that you have that ring, I need to tell you how important it's been to all the lives of the woman in our family. Did you know a sapphire stands for mental clarity and divine guidance, and rings represent eternal love? Ancient people believed that wisdom is contained within the gemstone. It's alleged that when the wearer of a sapphire faces challenging obstacles, the stone's power releases dreams of the consciousness that lead to clarification. There's a lot of history behind that heirloom you're wearing."

"I never thought a simple ring could mean so much."

"We've been passing along that ring for a long, long time. I know of only a few stories that my mom—your great grandmother—told me. One of the tales involved my mother's great-great-grandmother. She'd married young, and they were both hotheads. After a bad fight, her husband left her. The lady was all alone, abandoned in the town where they had rented a home. Things were different back then, with few employment opportunities for women. And divorce was unacceptable for decent folk. For days, she cried, wondering what was going to happen while her food dwindled and her prospects grew dreary. No one would hire her. The landlord was banging down the door."

"Couldn't she have returned home to family?"

"She didn't even have the money for that, and she missed the man she loved."

"He was horrible to leave her like that."

"A week later, she turned to the only help she had—the Lord. She owned an old tattered Bible her mother had given her. It was the first time she had even bothered to open the pages. She poured out her heart to God. The story says she stayed on her knees for hours, asking Jesus to bring back her husband and restore the love he once had in his heart. Her husband returned a short time later. He told his wife he had a number of dreams about her and realized he couldn't go on without her. Sometime later, they moved to a new town and lived together for forty-five years before she died."

"In this day and age, that gentleman would have come home to find the locks changed. But what does that have to do with the ring?"

Granny bypassed that question by holding up one finger. "There was another account of one of the women in the family. Her husband was in a bad accident, with no hope of living. His brother was a faithful man and lifted the sibling up in prayer every night. When she soon also started to believe that God was the only hope, she sought the Lord in prayer. Several weeks passed with her clinging to God and faith. The doctors couldn't believe it when her husband awoke. Of course, he faced months of recovery. He had to learn to walk and talk again. He later told her that when he was in the hospital in a coma, he had visions of her waving to him and reaching for his hand. Those images led him back to her."

"Incredible, Granny Kay."

"The most recent story I remember was my mother's. Right after she married my father, she started passing out. Months went by—sometimes she would lie sleeping for days, unable to wake up. She and Dad were afraid she might lose consciousness and never come around. The doctors couldn't find anything wrong. Mom explained to me how they both prayed, standing strong on God's word while waiting for a cure. One day, my mother was in the produce store and heard a man talking about a doctor in Raleigh. She started having dreams about searching for something in the house or garden. In them, see would find objects with this doctor's name written on them. Mother finally went to his office and made an appointment. He was a new and upcoming brain surgeon. A month later, he operated on her and removed a growth that was pressing against her brain. The physician told her she would have been dead in six months if he hadn't taken out the tumor. Two years after that, my brother Paul was born." Granny Kay sighed and took a sip of water. "Those are just a few of the stories that revolve around the ring."

Puzzled, Taylor glanced down at the floor then back at her grandmother. What was she trying to say? Those were interesting family accounts, but in none of them had there been any involvement of the ring. Sure, she felt goose bumps rise on her arms at the mention of the dreams—merely a coincidence.

Taylor grabbed hold of the stone that swung around her neck. "I still don't understand how any of those tales concern this ring."

Granny Kay smiled at her granddaughter. "You once told me you were experiencing some discomforting dreams. Can't you see? All those women wore that very ring that is hanging from your neck. That band has been prayed on so long that it's embedded with God's grace and mercy. On each occasion, those things worked out by faith and prayer."

Extending her hand, Granny Kay reached for Taylor and squeezed her hand. "I believe the dreams are a result of supplications to the Lord. Yes, some of the things that came to you may have seemed odd, but think about them. Often, dreams are our subconscious brought to life. Such imaginings, weird as they may seem at the time, cause folks to seek out other ways. They make people think about the outcome of their situations. In a way, many times dreams led the ladies in our family to the answers they were praying for in their lives. It wasn't ESP or magic. God created them."

"But I didn't pray for anything that would've brought on those dreams."

"Ever since you agreed to handle things at the house, Louise and I have prayed. We have called upon Jesus and stood on faith that you might find true happiness. I begged the Lord not to keep you in Panama."

"Granny Kay!"

"You have worn that ring from the first time it was found—you've had dreams also, just like our relatives. Prior to that, I don't believe you have ever had a history of restless sleeping." Setting up a little straighter in bed, she continued. "Tell me, when did those uneasy nights begin?"

Taylor sat motionless, thinking back to the times she woke up a nervous mess. She also recalled a few incidents when she had touched the stone and muttered a prayer or wished for something out of the blue. Without answering her grandmother, Taylor stood as if her seat had become hot. She had to get out of that room, away from the questioning eyes of her grandmother.

"Granny Kay, I'm going. You look tired, and it's been a long day. I'll talk to you tomorrow." She gave the older woman a quick peck on the cheek. Just as she reached the threshold of the door, she turned and made a final request. "Is it okay if I stay at the family home for a few nights?"

"Of course, dear. You know that house is as much yours as mine. Stay as long as you want."

Taylor marched out of her grandmother's door without looking back.

CHAPTER FIFTEEN

TAYLOR MADE A quick stop at Louise's house for her luggage. Then she veered off at a drive-thru burger joint. On her way to the property on Alder Court, she mulled over the things her grandmother had said. Could it be possible? Was God working to change her life?

Did He know what Taylor wanted better than she did?

Taylor pulled into the driveway of the family home and parked. For a moment, she just sat there. Her lips parted as she considered the odd stories her grandmother told. As much as she tried to dismiss them as rubbish, she couldn't. The eeriness of those accounts danced around in Taylor's mind, yearning to be recognized.

She placed her carryout on the kitchen table and walked into the guest room. After throwing her bag onto the bed, she walked into the adjacent bath. There she stood in front of the mirror, glaring at her reflection.

Was it true? Was God trying to lead her through those dreams? The idea seemed too unrealistic.

Her hand wavered as she took hold of the ring. Closing her eyes for a moment, Taylor debated removing the necklace and never putting it back on again. Her hand traveled to the hook that locked the chain. The reflection of the jewelry twinkled in the light.

Taylor's brow furrowed, and sensations swirled within her. Like the wind blowing a child's empty swing—back and forth, back and forth—she teetered between the urge to rip the necklace from her neck and to grab hold of the sapphire, giving in to all the desires she'd once buried. "Humph! I've had it on this long, and besides, the dreams have stopped. I'll just leave it alone, at least for now."

TAYLOR PICKED AT her food. Try as she might, she couldn't forget the incidents encircling the ring. She picked up a French fry and delivered it halfway to her mouth when the connection popped into her head. Yes, she remembered now. The beginning of her weird dreams *did* happen right after she slipped on the ring.

A song played on her phone, offering a distraction. Taylor sprang forward, dropping a piece of her food. She bent down and retrieved the fry from the floor, tossing it into a small metal trash can that sat upright in the corner, then grabbed her cell phone.

"Taylor, how is Kay?"

"Hi, Brent. She's doing fine. The doctor said she can go home next week."

Taylor listened to the hum of dead air, and then, as if he was trying to get the question out fast, he asked, "Will you find out soon whether you're going back to Panama?"

Sipping on her diet soda, she moved the straw with her lips. "My meeting with Mr. Zimmerman is tomorrow. The last time I spoke to him, well...he wasn't too happy that I came back to the States before I was scheduled."

"I understand. You have an important job. Sometimes, though, the ones we love precede everything else. We both know how dangerous a burst appendix can be—especially for an older person. God answered our prayers, but you could have lost her."

Taylor stood and chucked her bag of fast food into the small garbage can. "Yes, I know. There's no way I would have stayed there while she was in the hospital. But Mr. Zimmerman doesn't see it that way. To his way of thinking, Granny is fine, recovering, and I could have stayed in Panama and seen her in a couple weeks."

"He's wrong. One day he'll realize that. Hey..." The voice of the other end took on a lighter tone, changing the subject. "After the meeting with your boss is finished, can we go out tomorrow night?'

Taylor's lips curled in a smile. There was no denying the obvious—she cared for Brent Roberts, more than she had ever liked any man. *Liked...or loved?*

TAYLOR CARRIED HER breakfast with her as she walked into her grandmother's room. The two of them ate while they talked.

"I have a meeting with my boss after lunch. I guess I'll know then what happens at Mugful's."

"So you don't believe your boss will be sending you back to Central America?" Granny Kay eyed Taylor.

"I doubt it..." Shrugging, she took a sip of coffee. "He was very upset at me for coming home when I did." Without delay, she added, "I came back because I needed to. I love you."

As the older lady gazed at Taylor, her face a shade lighter, a look of sadness arose in her eyes. "I won't lie to you. I missed you very much and wanted you back home. Not at the expense of your job. I know your career means a lot to you. All I've ever prayed for was your happiness. It's worth a great deal to me."

TAYLOR MADE UP her mind to drop by and see Daisy before she headed to Raleigh to see Mr. Zimmerman. After all, she had a few minutes to spare, and soon Daisy would move away. She liked the older woman and enjoyed her company.

"How are you?" The middle-aged woman greeted her with a welcoming grin.

"I decided to stop over and say goodbye while I have the chance. Brent told me you were just about ready to leave."

"Yes, I'm turning the boutique over to the realtor next week, and I have hired a manager for the store. I'll be finishing up the sale of the house in a few days."

"It sounds exciting for you both."

Taylor strolled through the aisles of the shop, scanning the shelves. She watched Daisy's face shine with happiness as she expounded on her and her spouse's plans for the new life they were about to embark on.

"Oh my, yes. I'm so excited. A whole different adventure stands before us. It will be a tad hard to adjust—not working, that is. I'll treasure the rest of our lives together. Our anniversary is next month. I can't wait to celebrate the occasion in our new home, sitting on a balcony overlooking the ocean."

"Commitment like yours is a rare thing. You should be proud."

Daisy paused and patted Taylor's hand. "Dear, I hope you find someone to settle down with who will brighten your life the way my husband has mine. Oh, our marriage hasn't always been a bed of roses...or well...maybe it has. Roses are beautiful flowers. The petals are as gentle as silk, but underneath the splendor lay a few thorns. Either they're plucked off or avoided altogether."

Daisy moved to a rack and adjusted a dress that draped from a hanger. "I don't mind telling you that I had hopes for you and Brent. I know he likes you a lot. I've never seen him as excited over any woman as he is when he talks about you. Give him a chance. He's a decent man. He may be a little spoiled, but Brent's a good guy." Laughing, she added, "Even if he is my bratty baby brother."

TAYLOR SAT ACROSS from Mr. Zimmerman at his desk. He narrowed his eyes in contemplation as he touched the tips of his fingers together while resting his elbows on the mahogany desk. "You're a dedicated employee. But the unexpected trip home weakened my trust in you. The new beverage café in Panama is vital to this corporation. We have sunk a great deal of money into ensuring it surpasses the expectations of the tourists and the people of Central America."

"I understand and respect that."

"The agreement you and I had was that you would remain at the new facility, taking a three-day leave the month after the business had opened. You faltered, and that tested the dependence I placed on you."

Taylor pressed her back against the padded chair. She bit down on her tongue. Rebuttals circled around in her head. She wanted to protest, to defend herself. Although she was upset with his attitude, for some reason she backed off on the urge to be confrontational. Any statements Taylor made would only create more arguments.

Instead, she remarked, "Mr. Zimmerman, I can assure you I take my career very seriously. The only reason I jumped on an early flight was because of a desperate family situation. In all the years I have been employed at Mugful's, this incident was the first time I have gone against the company's wishes. It isn't something I did without a great deal of thought and remorse."

Leaning back in his leather chair, he eyed Taylor. "I'm in an awkward position. I feel it's in the best interest of the company to have Avery Thomas remain in Central America. That leaves me with another decision. The post you held in this office has been filled by your assistant, Dave. Over the years, that young man has shown much promise, so he was promoted. There isn't a place for you here now." Mr. Zimmerman paused and judged Taylor's reaction, speaking slower. "However, the office that Avery Thomas left in Virginia needs a manager. I haven't found a person I deem qualified to run that branch, so it's yours."

In a swift movement, he stood and straightened his chair. "I expect you to be ready to transfer to that facility within two weeks. That's as generous as I can be." Mr. Zimmerman turned in dismissal and put forth his last words. "Taylor, you are valuable to this company and have increased sales in this region. I trust that you will do the same with the branch in Virginia."

TAYLOR STORMED OUT of the building and seated herself in her car, slamming the door shut. She pressed her fingertips to her forehead at the tension headache forming. Her tongue hurt from gnawing at it to keep from slamming Mr. Zimmerman with every protest, every defense that had come to mind, but as she often heard her grandmother repeat, "Things spoken in anger are always regretted."

Contemplating the last few minutes of conversation with the president of the company, she fumed at how she'd been offered no choice. If she wanted to keep her job, Taylor was on her way to

Virginia. At least the state was only a few hours' drive from North Carolina, and the area was beautiful.

The only alternative to not moving was impossible. Quit her job and stay? How could she even consider it?

She veered into the traffic, headed to her condominium. Gripping the steering wheel, Taylor tried to reason with herself. "I do like the United States better than Central America. And Virginia's not far from North Carolina…"

TAYLOR PLANNED ON tossing her clothes in the washer and gathering a few more items before driving back to Liberty Cove. Of course, she could stay in her condo and travel the distance to see Granny Kay. For reasons Taylor didn't want to admit, something tugged at her to return to that small town. Back to the big house, the place where she spent so much time growing up. Her real home.

Hours later, Taylor grinned to herself as she tossed her clean clothes into the backseat of the vehicle. Despite it all, she was in a better mood. She slid into the driver's seat and repositioned the rearview mirror. While sorting through her mail and other odds and ends at her apartment, Taylor had put a few things into perspective—at least she hoped, anyway. As she started the vehicle, her musings returned to the conversation with her boss and the transfer.

What if…?

After stopping at the corner market to buy a cola, she headed toward the highway. The hour-long drive to the small town of Liberty Cove provided her with plenty of time to indulge in notions that demanded her attention and rethink her possibilities.

Her career had spiraled into a new dimension. The options seemed simple, even if her emotions were twisted in a knot.

Mugful's office in Virginia was in a large region, and she could see her grandmother any weekend. As for Brent, sometimes long-distance relationships worked.

Men... Why did caring for them have to be so complicated? Brent had her considering a time in the future—years to be exact. Where would she be then? Would she be dwelling in Virginia, working and slaving for Mugful's?

Taylor pulled into the circular drive of her large family home and turned off the ignition. She wanted to immerse herself in a hot bath before her date with Brent. She grasped the ring dangling from her neck. Eight months ago, she wouldn't have hesitated, would even be packing by now. That was before the remodeling of the house, prior to her meeting Brent Roberts. Prior to the ring.

AS BRENT AND Taylor waited for their meal in the restaurant, he studied her closely, sensing things weren't right. A strange look gleaming in Taylor's eyes bothered him—the same one she'd worn the day she announced she was going to Panama.

"I know you have something on your mind. What's up?"

"As you know, I talked to Mr. Zimmerman today. Basically, he informed me that since I returned from Central America, the only position left at Mugful's is at the Virginia branch. I have two weeks to move there."

Brent folded his arms across his chest and leaned back in the chair. His eyes searched hers, attempting to gauge how she felt about the new position. He didn't want to tether her, to take away her independence. He'd always like and respected her dedication, and he wouldn't do anything to hold her back.

The waitress approached and he waited for the young girl to refill their glasses with fresh tea before speaking.

"Taylor, I discovered a long time ago that life doesn't always end up the way we think it should. Often a door closes, but if we trust in the Lord, he will always open a window for us. I guess what I mean by that is you have other choices—*if* you think about it. You do what you need to." Brent reached out and touched Taylor's hand. "I'm not going anywhere. I love you. Who knows…maybe I need to open another Roberts Construction, one in Virginia."

"You'd do that?"

Brent placed his finger under her chin, planting a kiss on her lips. "Taylor Harrison, I love you, and if you move to Virginia and want me to, I will follow you."

TAYLOR LISTENED TO the birds sing in the early morning as she strolled down the walking path of Liberty Cove Memorial Hospital. Before stepping inside the entrance, she took a moment to soak in her surroundings. The night before, she had studied on her pending move to Virginia and replayed the chat she had with Brent. He loved her and was willing to move to be with her. Taylor should have told him how she felt, and indeed she'd tried when he took her home and kissed her goodnight. Somehow, though, the things she wanted to say stuck in her throat and refused to budge.

Now, she was letting herself admit the truth. She loved Brent and to her, loving a man was a serious pledge. Ever since she was a little girl, she'd promised herself that if she did make a commitment, it would be forever. The obligations her mom and dad shared, the love her grandmother and grandfather had sustained…both relationships appeared to be without an end. To her, that was what a woman and man did when together—devoted each day of their lives to one another.

Last night she'd realized something big—why her mother had chosen to trek around the country with her father. With all the traveling he did, they probably wouldn't be together today if her mother had stayed at home. Her mom enjoyed spending time with her husband. God had joined them together as one, and they couldn't bear to separate.

The dilemma of her move to Virginia no longer weighed so heavily. Her grandmother wouldn't be an issue. She was used to living an hour's drive from Taylor. Coming to see her from Virginia added only a few hours. It would be an easy Friday night or Saturday morning commute. In spite of all the positives she considered, somewhere hidden beneath the surface was the knowledge that she didn't want Brent to make changes. He was happy in this small town. His ties existed here in Liberty Cove, North Carolina. Did she want to split up his life that way?

Did *she* want to go?

KAY'S WORLD LIT up as her granddaughter walked through the door. "Hi, Granny Kay. I see you've had breakfast." Taylor nodded at the tray sitting on the metal stand. "The meeting with my manager was upsetting."

"Oh, no, dear. I'm sorry."

Taylor tucked a strand of hair behind her ear. "Basically, Mr. Zimmerman told me there isn't a position for me in the Raleigh office. So he has put me in charge of the branch that belonged to the man who took my place in Central America. I have two weeks to get settled as the manager in Virginia. At least the area isn't as far away as Panama. I can drive to North Carolina every weekend if I want."

This was a great day, as far as Kay was concerned.

Already, she had spoken with Louise. Her friend reported that Brent called and told her about Taylor, in secret of course, so Kay promised not to say anything.

Kay waited for her granddaughter to get to the good part, where she would tell her about Brent going along. She knew without a doubt that Taylor would visit every chance she had. The essential part was that Taylor and Brent would have each other.

She had prayed for Taylor to find true happiness in life and someone to share it with. If that meant her granddaughter would move to the state that bordered North Carolina, then so be it. At least it wasn't Central America. God had things under control. He delivered her only granddaughter back to the United States. He blessed her with love. Kay could accept small changes like this.

She smiled at that inspiration. The woman had lived long enough to believe that if God was on your side, things worked out. Kay planned to do her best to keep Jesus involved in Taylor's life. Prayers were powerful—if you believed and trusted in the Lord.

"Taylor, Virginia's not that far away. We can see each other often. You've always said how you enjoy driving that little sports car of yours."

They spoke about the doctor's latest report and the pending move. Finally, Taylor worked her way around to telling her about Brent offering to move with her. "Brent has said he wants to move with me to Virginia. He'll get his own apartment of course, but maybe we can find two condos in the same neighborhood or at least within a few miles of each other."

"That's wonderful. I suspected that young man had fallen in love with you. I see it in his eyes. Louise said he acted pitiful after you left and told him you didn't want to see him again."

The physician entered the room and informed them he planned on releasing Kay in the middle of the week. In his opinion, she had made full recovery, and despite the appendix episode, her health was good. His only advice was for her to relax for a while, not to lift or tug on anything. With humor in his voice, he added, "You don't need to be carrying heavy objects anyway. Leave that for the younger generation."

AFTER A SHORT conversation with Taylor, Brent slipped his cell phone in his pocket. His hand brushed the box from the jewelry store as his mind lingered on the decision he had made and what her answer might be—one that could change things forever. It was probably the biggest question he'd ever asked anyone. Even if she hadn't said as much, he believed in his heart that she loved him. Her kisses spoke volumes, certainly more than mere lust would. He wanted to shout his devotion to her from the roof tops.

Instead, he went to Daisy's Boutique to see his sister, swearing her to secrecy.

THE HOSTESS GUIDED them to their seats, passing by tall, hovering plants. Taylor scrutinized the elegant dining area. *Fancy, fancy...* She hadn't even realized this restaurant was close to Liberty Cove. The steakhouse was located just outside the city limits, right off the interstate. Brent spoke softly to the hostess when she offered them a table in the center of the dining area, and instead she led them both to a corner table at the far end of the room.

"This is a nice place. I see myself coming here again, maybe bringing Granny—if the food is good." Taylor watched Brent suspiciously. His mannerisms seemed off. He appeared nervous, not at all the self-assured man she was used to dealing with. As they sat at the corner table looking over the menu, Taylor asked, "Is everything okay? You're acting funny tonight."

Brent slipped his hand in his pocket and fiddled with the ring. "I think this restaurant has been here four years. They really do fix a good steak. This has just been a busy day. We had a mix-up on the materials at work, and later I went by Daisy's place. She's almost packed and ready to leave the end of the week. I'll miss my sister very much."

Even though Taylor heard what he was saying and believed without a doubt that he would wish to see his sister more often, those things didn't explain his uncharacteristic behavior. She chose to ignore his edginess for now, hoping it didn't have anything to do with his previous offer to follow her to Virginia. Had he changed his mind? About moving...about her?

After each of them had ordered a steak and the meal was presented, Brent spoke about Taylor's pending transfer. "I thought if you like, we could drive to your office in Virginia this weekend. Maybe check out the town. If I'm going to open another Roberts Construction, I'll need to see what spaces are available to rent. We both need to look at housing."

Taylor placed her fork on the plate and wiped her mouth. She glanced around at the restaurant, then again at Brent.

"What do you say?" His eyes seemed to sparkle.

He must be excited about this opportunity to expand his business. "That sounds fine to me, as long as Granny Kay is settled in with your aunt."

"I understand." Brent nodded and smiled. "Later in the week, we'll make more plans. I'm sure Louise and Kay will be fine with us going away for the day."

During the rest of the meal, Taylor relaxed for the first time since her meeting with the head of Mugful's. So what if she moved? Relocating to the next state over wasn't bad. She could see Granny Kay any weekend, and Brent was clearly eager to accompany her.

Despite the easy feeling she had concerning her job, Taylor battled some nagging, indefinable concern. Something she couldn't put her finger on wasn't quite right. Her gut told her things were off somehow. Was this the route her life should take?

LATER THAT NIGHT, they stood on the porch of the huge old home that had been in her family for generations, and Brent held her in his arms. His lips took her mouth and she responded with a passion all her own, totally immersed in the heat of the moment. He wrapped his arms around her. Brent's actions sealed off any misgivings she had about the future.

His passionate kiss drowned out the worries that lingered deep in her soul. Taylor's heart belonged to Brent. She understood now what Granny Kay meant about God working things out.

Needing to say the words, Taylor broke away. She inhaled gusts of air that came out in broken breaths, and her voice sounded shaky as she spoke. "It's time to be honest with you and myself. I love you." She sealed her statement with a kiss, feeling as if a huge burden had been lifted, then added, "Would you like to come in for a while? We can talk more about traveling to Virginia over a glass of tea. I can give you the directions to the office there. "

In awed silence, Brent thanked Jesus for her admission of love and the invitation to come inside. Both of these were things he wanted. "You know I love you too. Let's go inside."

As they walked into the foyer, Brent surprised her by requesting that they pour the drinks together. Once inside the room that now sparkled with new cabinets and granite counter tops, he backed her up to the sink, grinning like a child in a candy store. Again, he kissed her. This time it was long, lingering, and gentle.

When he finally released her, he stood in front of her. His eyes searched her face.

"I remember the first time I saw you. It was right here in the kitchen." He let out an easy laugh. "Then, Taylor, that day I saw you standing on the counter, when you dropped into my arms...in that moment you began to melt my heart. I'll never forget the look in those beautiful eyes. I was hurt when I thought you were gone from my life for three years. At the same time, I had to trust God, figuring the Lord would make a way if He meant us to be together."

"It would seem He did."

"I'm sorry that Kay got sick. I didn't want you to come back because of something bad. I guess Jesus was handling that also. He planned all along for your grandmother to get well. I only want us to be together forever." Brent slipped his hand into his pocket. Then he pulled out a shiny object that would barely fit on his pinky.

Taylor stared at him. Her mind circled round and round the words he spoke. She ogled the white-gold band with the pear-shaped diamond resting on top.

Brent took hold of her hand and slid the ring on her finger.

"I wanted to propose to you here, in this kitchen—the first place I laid eyes on the one lady who managed to steal my heart completely. Will you do me the honor of being my wife?"

Taylor moved her right hand to her face, rubbing her mouth. For what seemed like forever, she looked intently at the ring perched on the finger of her left hand. Then, certain of what she wanted, she answered. "I wasn't expecting this...yes. Oh, yes. I will marry you."

NEWS TRAVELED THE airwaves like lightning that night. Taylor called her grandmother in the hospital to share the proposal. Kay could barely press the numbers fast enough as she dialed Louise's phone. After that, Kay contacted her son. She knew Taylor should be the one telling her father and mother, but Kay felt as if she had a right—after all, it was her long hours of prayers that had gotten her granddaughter to this point.

Across town, Daisy was congratulating Brent.

It was after one in the morning before Taylor lay down. She was more excited than she ever could have imagined. She never fathomed that she would be this happy about her engagement, but she had no qualms about marrying Brent. This was what she wanted.

She drifted off to sleep as pictures played through her mind, fantasies of herself walking down the aisle, mental pictures of Brent, standing in his tuxedo, waiting for her.

As Taylor slept, vivid imaginings danced around in her subconscious. Interpretations of a new life to come drew her in and beckoned her to understand that happiness often originates from directions not expected.

While Taylor dreamt, revelations showed her a place all of her own, giving her spirit a taste of the happiness that could be hers. Taylor had only to grab hold of those opportunities and seize the new beginning that called to her.

TAYLOR WOKE WITH a start. She lay in the bed, glancing around the guest room, adjusting to her surroundings. This bedroom had undergone an update. New coats of paint shone, making the area appear much bigger. The carpet was ripped out, replaced by hardwood. The new floors gleamed, and the morning light beamed through the modern double-pane window—all Brent's handiwork.

Yes, everywhere in the Harrison house, reminders of Brent could be found. His construction talent was what had made her admire the big place so much. The changes Brent made in the dwelling had shown Taylor that things weren't always as they seemed. Sometimes the answer lies under the surface.

All these years she thought of this house as a huge problem. Now, she took away a different impression. No longer did these walls seem an ill fit to her idea of life. Yes, the residence would continue to be huge, yet inside those walls, an aura of love and coziness existed.

As she rose from bed, her thoughts staggered to another truth she'd discovered last night. Indeed, her grandmother was right—sometimes dreams can direct a person if they take the time to pay attention.

TAYLOR HEADED TO the bathroom and eyed her likeness in the mirror. The ring that hung on a chain around her neck sparkled in the lighted space. Taylor touched the stone. Her lips extended in a smile. She stepped closer to the reflection and inspected the gem. Yes, this was a special piece of jewelry. *It sure has changed my life.*

She turned on the shower. Eagerness filled her soul in anticipation of the events she had planned…if her day worked out. She couldn't be more excited. Now she had knowledge of the very direction she wanted her future to take. As she stood in the shower and lathered her hair, she mumbled to herself, "Who would believe that Taylor Harrison was on the verge of changing things to such an extreme?"

TAYLOR MADE THE necessary phone calls. Snatching up her pocketbook, she headed to the door. It took forty-five minutes on the telephone to work out the details. Her appointments were all set. If everything went according to plan, by evening she would celebrate a new life.

First, she had to visit her grandmother in the hospital, and then she would have lunch with Daisy. Later, Taylor intended to call Mr. Zimmerman. For now, she had more important things on her mind.

"TAYLOR, HONEY, COME here." Granny Kay stretched out her arms to embrace her granddaughter. "I was certain you and Brent were supposed to be together. I'm so happy you two are getting married. Have you set a date?"

Taylor grinned at her grandmother's excitement. "No, we haven't gotten that far yet. I promise it will be soon."

During the next hour, Kay chatted with her granddaughter about the pending ceremony. Taylor wanted to a church wedding and agreed her grandmother could tell Pastor Grant about the engagement.

A short while later, Taylor stood, lifting her purse to her shoulder. She walked to the hospital bed.

"Granny Kay, I've made some decisions regarding my life. I have several meetings to attend to today, so I need to leave. I won't be back until tomorrow."

"Everything is okay?"

"It's all good. I have lots to do. If what I have planned works out, I promise you will be happy."

Kay Harrison chuckled at Taylor's enthusiasm and waved her hand in the air, dismissing her. "Go on then and we will talk later. I get to go home in two days, anyway."

As Taylor strode to the exit, Kay called after her, "I can't tell you how fortunate I feel. Not only did I get you back, but I'll soon have a nice-looking young man in the family."

TAYLOR AND DAISY SPENT most of the day together. After lunch, they met at Liberty Cove Notary, signing and officiating large amounts of paperwork. Taylor's new life awaited.

Now, Daisy stood beside her car, shuffling things around in her purse as she gathered the keys to the dress shop and handed them over the new owner.

"I'm glad you bought the shop, and I'm even happier that you and my brother are getting married. I'm looking forward to coming back for the wedding and having you as my sister-in-law."

"I'm sure I'll enjoy the boutique as much as you have over the years. I can't wait to get started. Will you do me a favor, though? I want to surprise Brent. Call him Friday morning and ask him to come by the mini-mall. Just don't mention my name or any of this."

GRANNY KAY PEEPED out the door of Taylor's car at Louise's place. Taylor honked the horn, and Louise appeared at the door, swinging it open. "Hi, Kay! Welcome home."

Taylor and Louise walked with Granny Kay into the house. "It's good to be out of that dreadful hospital." She seated herself in a living room chair, leaning her head back on the suede material. "Taylor, when are you going to Virginia?"

Taylor sat in a chair across from her grandmother and stared at the floor. She didn't want to lie. All she wanted was to keep the plans quiet and surprise Brent.

"Can you and Louise keep a secret for a day?"

Kay and Louise gave each other long looks and then nodded their heads in absolute agreement.

"I've bought Daisy's Boutique. I'm staying in Liberty Cove and if Brent agrees, I want us to live in the Harrison estate." Taylor stood and closed the distance between herself and her grandmother, stooping down to take the older woman's hand in hers. "Once Brent and I marry and move in, I want you to live there with us."

As Taylor hugged her grandmother goodbye and turned to leave, she pretended not to notice the puddle of tears in the corner of the older woman's eyes. Without a doubt, this time they came from unspeakable joy.

For once, without a single misgiving in her heart or mind, Taylor had made the right decision.

TAYLOR ARRIVED AT the boutique early. She laid out the notes she'd taken the night before, listing some changes she wanted to make. The manager Daisy hired had a few days off, thanks to Taylor. She wanted to take a week and do some reorganizing.

After she had rearranged a few displays, she climbed to the top of the wall shelf, closest to the front door. She positioned herself on the sliding ladder, which glided over the length of the top shelves. Several times, Taylor overextended her arm toward the sign she was attempting to remove. The door chimed, signaling that someone had entered. Taylor's foot slipped off the rail. She screamed as her body plummeted.

"Whoa!" Strong arms caught her. "Lady, we have to stop meeting like this."

After a moment's shock, she looked into Brent's eyes, remembering back months ago to another time when she had fallen into his arms.

In a bossy tone, she pretended annoyance. "Mr. Roberts, put me down this instant."

Brent's gaze raked over her with affection.

"Ms. Harrison, I'll never be able to let you go. I'm convinced we belong together." Nonetheless, he set her on her feet. "What's going on, Taylor? Why are you working in Daisy's dress shop?"

"Brent, I'm in *my* new boutique. I bought this shop from Daisy."

THE TWO OF them spent several hours in Taylor's new store. They talked about their upcoming wedding and the beginnings to come for the Roberts clan.

"Brent, I want us to attend church together on a regular basis. I have gotten stale in my religion. It's time I fix things with God and grow as a Christian."

Brent circled Taylor with his arms and whispered in her ear. "With the Lord on our side, you and I have some great journeys ahead."

She snuggled closer in his arms. "Speaking of wonderful expeditions, why don't we go to Panama for our honeymoon? I have a friend by the name of Brenda Stone. I want you to meet her."

Brent nodded. "Central America sounds like a good place to celebrate our marriage. I hope you don't mind if we get married soon. I can't wait to start my life with the woman I love."

Taylor pitched her head back and laughed. "That's fine with me." Her voice changed, sounding serious. "How would you feel about the two of us living at the Harrison home…with my grandmother?"

Brent adored this woman. He stood close to her, relishing her scent, her voice, her dedication—now to him and her family. He promised himself that he would spend the next fifty years appreciating and spoiling her. "I can't think of anything I'd want more. And with all that space, there are plenty of accommodations." After he planted a kiss on her lips, he stepped back and added, "Who knows, maybe we can work on filling up more of those empty rooms. That house was built for laughter and playful sounds."

CHAPTER SIXTEEN

"Darling, you look exquisite."

"Thanks, Granny Kay. I believe I'm ready to walk down the aisle." Taylor adjusted the train of her gown and then took one last glimpse of her necklace in the mirror. Just as her face glowed with happiness, the ring also glistened, as if sending its own stamp of approval on what was about to occur.

Taylor's father stood at the door that led to the church. "Well, I hear your cue. Let's get this show on the road, young lady."

As her dad held out his arm for Taylor, Granny Kay wiped a tear from her face and kissed her granddaughter's cheek. "I'm going to sit down. The next time I talk to you, I will be speaking to Mrs. Brent Roberts."

Brent stood still as Taylor approached. All he could think about was how beautiful she was. Even though the dress was a unique, striking blend of silk and beads, to him the clothing wasn't what made his bride attractive. It was her spirit that shone beautiful.

Brent held his nervous jitters at bay while he turned to face his wife-to-be. The words he spoke to her over the next ten minutes were all that mattered.

Taylor took her place beside her soon-to-be husband. With shaking hands, she repeated the vows. The last few minutes seemed like hours. She was ready to have the kind of commitment her parents and grandparents had held fast to all these years.

When the last announcement came—the one addressing them as Mr. and Mrs. Brent Roberts—the couple marched down the aisle.

Taylor grinned like a fool, unshakably happy for a girl who hadn't wanted a serious relationship. Oh, she and Brent would have their moments. Taylor loved this man with all her heart. He was a bit cocky at times with his "don't worry, it'll work out" attitude and, of course, she was one to stress too much.

Yes, a few challenges might lie ahead. She believed this was the path God intended her to walk. The joy or sadness awaiting in their lives no one other than God could see.

The last thought had her rubbing the stone of the infamous ring, a precious stone that held the prayers of generations of her relatives. She was sure hers would be added in the years to come.

CHAPTER SEVENTEEN

TAYLOR AND BRENT explored the streets of Central America. "Taylor, you were right. This is a diverse city. The architecture is something to see." He hugged Taylor, backing her up alongside a building. "I wouldn't trade this moment for anything."

Taylor's face lit as she kissed him. In the most provocative voice she could muster, she said, "Down, boy. We have years to be romantic with each other."

"Yes, I know. You can't blame a guy for seizing every opportunity he can to seduce his wife, can you?" Taylor laughed as Brent released her and they continued strolling down the street to the La Posta restaurant.

"I'm starved. I sure hope they have something a regular guy from North Carolina will enjoy."

Taylor looked sideways at Brent and snickered. "Brenda and I ate here a couple times. The food is good." Looking ahead in the crowd, she spotted her friend taking a seat at a corner table. "I believe we arrived on time."

A few moments later, the waiter led them to their seats.

"It's good to see you again, Taylor. This must be Brent."

Taylor sat in the chair Brent offered and proceeded to introduce the two. "Brenda, this is Brent, my husband."

Placing her napkin in her lap, Brenda made a declaration. "Even though I miss you around here, I'm glad you finally came to your senses and grabbed hold of love. Also, I hear you have a new enterprise."

Taylor sheepishly glanced in Brent's direction and then back at her friend. "I have to confess to you that you were right—I was a little scared. I know how to run a company. That's easy. Sometimes, life is a whole lot more complicated than any business transaction could ever be."

"And sometimes we're the cause of that complication."

Taylor smiled. "I'm going to enjoy every minute of the dress shop. I take pleasure in helping the customers. When I was young, I enjoyed working in a store. Over the years, I forgot that sometimes the greatest satisfaction comes from the simple things."

During the next hour and a half, they talked of each other's lives, laughed about situations that happened in the office, and compared differences between Central America and the United States. At the end of the dinner, Brenda made Taylor promise to keep in touch. Brent shook the woman's hand, and both ladies exchange hugs and goodbyes.

EPILOGUE

"MOMMY, AREN'T YOU suppose to work today?"

Taylor reluctantly kneeled to the floor so she could be at eye level with her daughter, her huge abdomen barely allowing the action.

"No, dear, I'm letting my assistant take care of the dress shop while we're gone. Bianca, remember Mommy told you that you, Daddy, and I are going to Aunt Daisy's for a few days? Go say goodbye to Granny Kay and get your doll. Daddy's loading the car."

Five-year-old Bianca placed her hands on her tiny hips and gazed at her mother. "Mommy, when are you going to the hospital to bring my brothers home?"

Taylor laid her hand on her belly. "Honey, it will be three more months before the twins come."

The inquisitive child with a slightly crooked grin reached out and touched the sapphire ring that hung from her mother's neck. "This is pretty. Where did you get it?"

Taylor looked at her little girl with admiration, smoothing back her dark blonde hair as thoughts of finding the ring and events of the past seven years ran amuck in her mind.

"This is an extraordinary ring that has belonged to many generations of our family." Taylor fingered the blue stone. "This ring is full of love and prayers, and one day you will have it."

Brent stepped inside the kitchen door and heard Taylor talking to their daughter. As he marched over to help his pregnant wife stand, he commented, "Yes, Bianca, the gem Mommy wears is very special. Thanks to the prayers your ancestors offered when they had it, this ring is a symbol of hope, love, and the power of faith." Brent bent down and scooped his daughter into his arms. "The pretty blue stone represents devotion and Heaven. You remember Heaven is what Pastor Grant has been teaching us about." Brent reached out and fingered the stone. "The sapphire is called the Stone of Destiny. For Mommy and me, the ring simply reminds us we need to have faith in God.

"One day, Bianca, this will be your ring. Always remember that a piece of jewelry isn't what makes us happy or changes lives. Ultimately, it's your relationship with Jesus Christ."

ABOUT THE AUTHOR

Mary L. Ball enjoys writing inspirational suspense and mystery novels blended with romance. She's a member of ACFW and lives in North Carolina between the wondrous mountains and beautiful beaches. When she's not immersed with fictional characters, she enjoys her family, church, and the outdoors. Visit her at: http://MaryLouwrites.weebly.com.

Thank you for your Prism Book Group purchase! Visit our website to enjoy free reads, great deals, and entertaining, wholesome fiction!

http://www.prismbookgroup.com

Made in the USA
Columbia, SC
19 September 2023

23076615R00115